COUSINS IN DEVON

by

AMY LE F

LUTTERWORTH PRESS
LONDON

PRINTED IN GREAT BRITAIN
BY EBENEZER BAYLIS AND SON, LIMITED
THE TRINITY PRESS, WORCESTER, AND LONDON

CONTENTS

CHAPTER   PAGE

1 AUNT JUDY   7

2 THE FERRY HOUSE   17

3 COUSIN HARRY   30

4 A RAMBLE ON THE MOOR   40

5 BABS AS HOUSEKEEPER   53

6 BEE AND HER PONY   66

7 COUSIN TED'S STORY   77

8 A DARTMOOR GALE   92

9 MRS. PERCIVAL'S GUEST   107

10 THE PICNIC   119

11 HARRY'S NEWS   130

12 DISASTER ON THE MOOR   142

CHAPTER ONE

AUNT JUDY

BABS, Bob and Bee were having their breakfast. Fanny, the maid of all work, had brought in three saucers of porridge, and had told them to "sit up at the table proper, and be'ave theirselves, for their pore ma were up till midnight sortin' out papers, and were near worn out with all she 'ad to do."

Babs was about to speak, but the door opened, and like a fresh sunny breeze, Mrs. Percival swept into the room.

She was a very young mother, and a widow. The children's father, a clergyman, had died about a month previously.

She beamed upon her children as if she were just seeing them for the first time that morning.

"Well, darlings, here I am," she said. "Have you heard of Aunt Judy? She is coming to see us this morning."

"We've never heard of her," cried Babs; and Bob and Bee echoed her words.

"No, I suppose not. She's almost a stranger

to me, but she's your father's sister. I wonder if I had better tell you about her?"

"Oh do, Mums," said Bob earnestly; "we've never had an aunt before."

His mother looked at him gravely.

"I often warn you against quarrelling, chicks; for if you start any habit when you're young, it doesn't leave you when you grow old. Your Uncle Ralph quarrelled with your father just before I married, and Aunt Judy took his side, and she has never taken any notice of us since. Now she says that she is sorry, and she is coming to see us, and we must hurry with our breakfast, for I shall have to help Fanny to get a nice lunch for her."

The children were much excited at the prospect of seeing a new aunt. They were a happy trio; the two little girls were fair haired and blue eyed, the boy brown eyed, with a crop of curly auburn hair, and freckled across his nose. They were much the same height, and there was barely a year between them. Babs tried to control her younger brother and sister, but Bee was more rebellious than Bob, for she had a stronger personality.

There was quite a little bustle in their quiet house that morning. It was raining fast, so though Mrs. Percival sallied forth in her old mackintosh to do some necessary shopping, the children stayed at home, and tried to help Fanny in preparing for the visitor.

"I wish we were rich!" sighed Babs, resting after her efforts, and pressing her nose against the window pane with a disconsolate face; "Mums would be able to give Aunt Judy such a lovely dinner if we were."

"What's it going to be?" enquired Bob anxiously.

"Oh, Bob, there's a taxi stopping, and a tall, a very tall lady getting out, and looking up at the house! What shall we do? Mums is out, and she's come too early, and we haven't tidied ourselves."

A sharp ring at the bell proclaimed the visitor. They heard a very pleasant hearty voice in the hall say, "Oh I'll come in, and wait. I should like to see the children," and the next moment Fanny ushered in Miss Judith Percival.

Babs stood up and held out her small hand.

"How do you do," she said in best imitation of her mother's manner, "how good of you to come to see us! Do sit down. What a wet day!"

Miss Percival had a sense of humour. She was a handsome woman, with fresh complexion, dark eyes and a happy contented face.

"And so you're my eldest niece! Well, I'm disappointed not to find your mother in, for I'm lunching the other side of London this morning. Won't you give me a kiss?"

9

Babs advanced to obey, but Bob called out in remonstrance.

"Oh, but Mums and Fanny are getting ready lunch for you, and Mums has gone to the butcher's for the meat."

"She won't be long," said Babs, frowning upon Bob for his indiscreet revelation. Then she re-seated herself and remarked confidently to her aunt:

"Bob and Bee don't know how to make conversation, but I do."

"Well, I don't," said her aunt bluntly; "and I'd like to see you all. Where's the other one?"

"I'll fetch her," and Bob raced from the room.

"Come here, little woman, I'm your aunt, and I don't want to be treated like a visitor."

Babs came towards her aunt, and felt a kind motherly arm encircle her.

"Don't you go to school?"

"No, Mums teaches us when she can, but I'm going soon. At least I was, but now Mums says, the skies seem to have tumbled on us, and we're all upset and anyhow!"

Miss Percival regarded her small niece reflectively.

"I ought to have known you sooner. It's my own fault. Don't be proud and unforgiving, Babs, it leads you into dreadful straits and you lay up remorse for yourself for ever."

The door opened, and Bob appeared, pushing Bee before him. She went to her aunt at once, and put up her face to be kissed. Aunt Judy began to enjoy herself. She had a natural love for children and understood them. Why had she not, she asked herself, made acquaintance with these little ones before?

When Mrs. Percival returned from the shops a quarter of an hour later, she found her children clustered round their aunt, talking to her as if they had known her all their lives. Miss Percival met her sister-in-law very calmly.

"Well, Edie, better late than never, this is my tardy excuse. I've come to see if I can help you with plans. You won't go on living here, will you?"

"Not in this house," said Mrs. Percival quietly. "I'd like to get out of London. But where can we go?"

"Well, I could offer you a home, but I've only a small establishment—still——"

"The last people in the world with whom I'd live would be any of my husband's relations," said Mrs. Percival emphatically.

Miss Percival laid her hand on her arm.

"My dear, let us bury the past. I wrote to you, and I can write better than I can speak. I'm not one to reiterate apologies. Now let us sit down and have a confab!"

They were left alone, and they talked long and earnestly for a good hour. The children sat on the kitchen table and talked hard to Fanny.

"I think she's a kind of fairy godmother," said Babs; "she's got such grand furs round her, and looks like a queen."

"She may be going to give Mums enough money to let us go over to Ireland to Mums' old home, which was sold. She could buy it back and let us live there for ever," suggested Bob.

"Now you go off to the dining-room all of you," Fanny said, "and I'll may be drop a pudding in the pot, with a bit of jam runnin' through it!"

The children screamed with delight, then danced off to the dining-room. Then they plunged into an exciting game of being wrecked on a desert island.

The table was the island, and Bob sailing by (on a cushioned chair) rescued his sisters from starvation, but chained them up as slaves, putting them into the hold of his ship. (This was a small toy cupboard in the corner of the room.) They were just about to burst their bonds, break open the prison door, and pursue him up and down his quarter deck with two sharp sabres, when they heard their mother's summons calling them to wish their aunt goodbye.

They came out into the hall with ruffled

heads of hair and with panting breath. Miss Percival laughed at them.

"Goodbye, little ones. Tell your mother if she doesn't do what I want her to do, she'll be sorry for it one day! Write to me soon."

She was gone, and Mrs. Percival followed her children back into the dining-room with a dazed dreamy look in her eyes.

"What is it she wants you to do?" enquired Babs at once.

"I think she's rather nice," said Bob.

"I love her," exclaimed Bee.

Mrs. Percival laughed.

"It's rather a bolt from the blue! I shall have to think about it. You mustn't worry me, chicks. I'll tell you when I've decided tomorrow. Now get your lesson books; I'll run out to Fanny first, and then we must give our attention to lessons."

The children did as they were told, but when their mother left the room, their tongues were busy.

"Aunt Judy lives in a big house and we're all going to live with her," announced Babs with conviction in her tone.

"And she may keep rabbits," said Bob. "I do wish somebody *really* rich would buy me a rabbit. They're *so* cheap to feed, they don't want milk like cats do."

"She may possibly have a tree in her garden,

big enough to have birds' nests in with eggs,"
said Bee.

This flight of imagination made Bob caper
round the room.

"Trees, a lot of trees which we can climb!
What does Mums want to think about, I wonder!
I wish we could go off tomorrow."

"She's going to ask God what He thinks," said
Babs softly. "She always does what He tells her."

For the rest of that day their new aunt was
the principal topic of their talk. When bedtime
came, Babs asked her mother if she couldn't tell
them a little more.

"Just to dream of," she begged. "We want to
know what kind of a house she lives in, and
whether we're going to live with her."

"Little curiosity," said her mother, playfully
pinching her ear. "But I can relieve your mind
on this point. We are *not* going to live with her.
She did suggest it, and would have been glad to
have us all I really believe, but I said, 'No, no,
no, thank you!' "

"Why, Mums?"

A feeling of disappointment crept over Babs.

"Because, darling, I'm an old-fashioned
mother. I will have a home of my own, however
small it is, and I want no one else's."

Babs got into bed with a sigh.

"I thought she looked rich, and would have a

14

big house, and then we could have been rich too."

"Oh, my darling, don't think that being rich makes you happy. Rich people are often unhappy and disagreeable. They can't enjoy things as we do, as it is so difficult to surprise them. We all love surprises, don't we?"

"Oh yes, they're derlicious!" assented Babs. "I hope it will be a nice surprise tomorrow, Mums, when you tell us."

"We'll hope so."

Mrs. Percival spoke absently. She folded up her children's clothes, then gave her goodnight kiss to each of them.

"Anyhow, wherever we are, and wherever we go," she assured them, "we shall be happy, because God will be with us, loving and caring for us."

And then she went downstairs leaving them to sleep, and spending the rest of the evening with her work basket, darning well-worn socks and mending various small garments.

Underneath her breath she hummed a little song to herself with words like these:

"Overhead a blue sky,
   Under foot a rough road,
But the roughness leads to the blue,
   Overhead One who cares,
Underneath are the tears,
   But the overhead Father loves you."

And then Fanny broke in upon her solitude.

"If you please'm, there be no eggs left, and the beastly cat have crept into the larder and made h'off with the last bit o' bacon."

Mrs. Percival's merry laugh rang out.

"Never mind, Fanny; porridge and jam for breakfast for all of us. We might have worse fare."

Fanny departed to her kitchen again.

"Never seed anyone get a laugh out o' misfortunes as she do, and if this 'ere surmise of the children be true, and we be goin' to 'ave a move out of London, I'm goin' to stick to the family, sure as h'eggs be eggs! For never shall I get another missis like 'er!"

Later on when Fanny had gone upstairs, Mrs. Percival remained in the sitting-room. She was sitting with hands clasped round her knees gazing into the dying embers of her fire, and wondering and praying over the new chapter in life which seemed to have been brought to her by Aunt Judy.

CHAPTER TWO

THE FERRY HOUSE

"NOW Mums, tell us."

Three expectant faces were raised to their mother's rather grave countenance.

Breakfast was over. Babs had helped her mother make the beds. Bob had blacked his own shoes, Bee had dusted the little drawing-room. The meals for the day had been arranged, and now Mrs. Percival sat in her chair at the small dining-table. It was the time for lessons, but she had told the children that she was going to give them a holiday this morning.

"Well, I have thought it over, and I am going to do what Aunt Judy wishes. It will mean giving up our kind friends here, and starting a new home amongst strangers. But it will be a healthy life and a happy one for you. And I think on the whole it will give us more comfort, for I shall have no house rent to pay, and shall have more money for our needs."

"Why, Mums, it will be ever so nice, why do you look so sad?" And Babs seized hold of her mother's hand and laid it caressingly against her cheek.

"I want your father badly," said Mrs. Percival with tears in her eyes, which she vainly tried to control. "And it doesn't seem loyal to him to be taking this house, and going to live so near his old home. I can't explain things to you, my chicks. It is best not, but your father was misunderstood, and though it is all found out now, when he is gone, I can't forget, and it is too late for him. He is gone."

"But God will tell him all about it," said Babs wisely.

Mrs. Percival dried her tears and began to smile again.

"And now I'll tell you about our new home. It will be in Devonshire, the prettiest county in England, and it's called the Ferry House, for it is by a narrow bit of river. I shall have to teach you all to swim, for I can't have you falling in the river, and getting drowned. There is no ferry man now. He died two years ago, and a bridge has been built across the river, so there is no ferry boat required. It is a cottage belonging to your aunt, it is part of her property, and she thought of us when she heard that we should be obliged to move out of our present house. It is quite in the country, one way across the bridge leads to the village, the other way up to a moor. I know it well, for your father and I often used to ride across by the ferry and go up to the moor."

"Tell us how many rooms and cupboards, Mums."

"And shall we have a boat of our own?"

"And shall we catch fisses in the river?"

"I think there are four rooms, a big kitchen, and a tiny parlour. I don't know how many cupboards there are, but I do know that we shall have to be very tidy, for it will be a much smaller house than this. We shall have no boat, and I don't want you to spend your time close to the water. I shall send you off to the woods and moor."

"Oh, Mums, woods!"

When once it was settled, events moved fast. Some of the furniture had to be sold; only the smallest pieces could be taken down to the cottage. There was much correspondence between Mrs. Percival and Aunt Judy. Then one day she went down, and slept a night with her sister-in-law. When she came back, she looked happy and relieved in mind.

"Aunt Judy is so kind, she is papering the cottage and painting it, and making it all so pretty. I really think we shall be very cosy in it," she said. "And we are turning the little parlour into the kitchen and going to have the big kitchen for our sitting-room. And there's a nice garden and two apple trees in it. And it is quite above the river. You go up steps to get into the garden. It's very old and quaint, and has a lot of cupboards. And a great big oven for baking bread next the fire place, big enough to bake each one of you."

"P'raps an ogre once lived there," said Bee with round eyes.

"Perhaps!" laughed her mother.

As the house got more and more uncomfortable with the packing, the children grew happier and happier.

And when it came to the last day but one, and they sat on the floor and ate their food off a wooden box, it was the height of their enjoyment.

When they were at last off in the train with all the houses, and chimneys, and smoke, disappearing behind them, and the fresh green country with its pure sweet air blowing in at the carriage windows, Mrs. Percival sat looking out in dreamy content.

Then she put her arms round Bob and drew him to her.

"You're the man of the family, my Bob, so I shall try and bring you up to be a farmer."

"And what shall I be?" enquired Babs.

"Yes, darling, you shall be a market gardener and grow fields of daffodils and violets."

Babs danced up and down in her seat at the thought of it.

"And me?" questioned Bee.

"Oh *you*," said her mother as she gathered her into her arms, "you shall have a chicken farm, and watch the chicks come out of their eggs. And your old mother will toddle round and visit you all, and you must each have an arm chair ready and waiting for her!"

When they reached the little station of Moorcombe they found that Miss Percival had thoughtfully sent a private motor-bus for them. The children were now so excited that they could not keep still, but they were not far from the little village, which stood on the crest of a hill, its ivy-towered church in the midst of it; and then going down a narrow lane they came to a grey stone bridge over a brown rushing river. Upon the other side on a green knoll with pine-trees at the back stood the old ferry house. It was a quaint yellow cob cottage with old russet tiled roof, and casement windows.

The children darted up the steep flight of stone steps that led from the lane, and found themselves in a good sized front garden. A big lawn with apple trees at the bottom, and a long bed of flowering daffodils before the cottage windows confronted them.

"Oh," cried Babs, "isn't it too lovely, Mums?"

Bob tore to one side of the garden, and looked over the hedge.

"There are lambs in a field, are they ours?" he asked.

His mother shook her head, then she opened the house door. Miss Percival again had been busy inside. There was a bright wood fire in the old-fashioned kitchen, and the table was spread with a white cloth ready for tea. There was even a blue vase with some yellow daffodils in it in the centre of the table. The room was papered with a bright chintz paper, all the wood was dark brown; there was a door on one side of the fireplace disclosing a steep flight of wooden stairs leading to the bed-rooms above, another door led into the small parlour that was going to be made into a kitchen, and a third door led into the garden. Upstairs Mrs. Percival was to occupy the big room with her two little girls. There was a small room for Bob, one for Fanny, and another small room was going to be used as a box-room.

The sun was shining through a west window in Mrs. Percival's room, and she opened the window and leant out, drawing in deep breaths of the sweet country air. The lane went up to the moor on one side of the house; in front was the garden, the river, and the view of the distant village on the top of the hill; fields surrounded them at the back, and on the western side.

Fanny found the kettle boiling, and soon

Mrs. Percival was enjoying a cup of tea, and the children's tongues wagged fast between satisfying their hunger and expressing their opinions of their surroundings. Later on their mother turned them out into the garden to play.

It was an enchanting pastime to be able to scramble up into a real tree, and stay there, and as they were naturally very quick and agile, they found no difficulty in doing it. Each found a branch to sit upon, in one of the apple trees, and then from this vantage ground they could see over the garden hedges. The field of sheep and lambs so close to them proved most attractive.

"There's a gate into the field," said Babs; "we'll go and see them."

Down they scrambled, out of their garden gate, down the steep stone steps into the lane, then after a good deal of fumbling they managed to open the big gate into the field, and stole softly over the grassy field towards the sheep. Alas! it was not so easy to come near them.

The sheep were not accustomed to children, and began to run. Soon the whole flock was in motion, and then casting caution to the winds, the children tore after them. The chase was most exciting. They tried to get them up into one corner of the field, but it was beyond their powers. The feel of the short turf under their feet, the bracing moor air, and the delight of chasing animals, who were unable to hurt or harm them, made them forget everything but the joy of the moment. Suddenly an angry shout brought them to a standstill. A big stout man flourishing a stick in the air was striding across the field towards them.

"Here, ye young varmints! 'Ave done will 'ee, or I'll lay me stick along yer backs, certain sure I will!"

The children stopped running instantly, they stood together eyeing the approaching farmer with frightened eyes.

"How daur ye rin me sheep down! What be 'ee doing of in my field, a trespassin' an' a damagin' my property!"

"Please, we were only playing games with them," said Babs, who was always the spokeswoman. "We wouldn't hurt the darlings for the world!"

"Not for the worl'," echoed Bee. Then she rushed forward and clasped the farmer round the knees.

"Oh do catch one of the sweet little lambs, and let me pet it."

The rough farmer looked down at the sweet little face uplifted to his, and let his stick drop with a thud to the ground.

Then he scratched his head.

24

"Who be 'ee?" he asked. "But 'tis shameful work a harassin' an' fashin' of my sheeps! Doan't 'ee knaw 'tis destruction to 'un to race 'em roun' an' roun' in thiccy giddy fashion?"

"We live at the Ferry House," said Babs, advancing with more composure now the stick was out of the stranger's grip, "and we've just walked in to make friends with your sheep, only they will run away. We're very sorry if running is bad for them, but we love running ourselves, and dogs and cats don't take harm from running, so we didn't know. We won't do it again."

"No," put in Bob, "we'll go home at once. Can you tell us what animals run in the country, because we don't want to make mistakes? I'm sure rabbits do—I s'pose you don't know where the rabbits live? I should like to have one of my own so much."

They were standing round the farmer now, eager to make friends with him. Bee even picked up his stick and handed it to him. His anger passed. He took them back to the gate, but sternly told them that he would rather they kept out of his field for the future, and they promised they would do so. When they returned to their apple-trees, they began pondering over this.

"I thought all the fields were free," said Babs.

"They ought to be in the country," said Bob.

"Does every field belong to somebody?" asked Bee.

At this moment Mrs. Percival came across the lawn. When she heard about the sheep, she shook her head at them.

"You must never chase any cattle," she said. "When dogs do it, they get shot. I'm sorry you've begun so badly. I want to be friends with the country people round us."

"Oh, he isn't very cross," said Babs, "it was only when he didn't know us. He says the Ferry House was a whist old place, when Tom Fagan lived there. What is whist, Mums?"

"It's a Devon word. Ask your aunt. And now come in and have some supper and go to bed. I shall be glad of my bed tonight and so will Fanny. But we're fairly straight now."

Very soon there was a hush and quiet in the old Ferry House.

The children were out of bed very early the next morning. Spring was in the air, the sun was shining; apple blossom seemed to have opened out in the night, and to their great regret they were told by their mother that they must not make the trees their playground.

"If you knock this early bloom off, we shall have no apples. Don't climb the trees, play about on the grass as much as you like."

"I thought there were no 'don'ts' in the

country," said Bob a little rebelliously; "it's as bad as the parks in London. We're *not* to go into the fields and we're *not* to climb trees; what is there we can do?"

His mother laid her hand on his shoulder.

"You can help me in a lot of ways today," she said cheerfully; "life isn't all play, Bob, and we have good times in front of us. There's a small box or two I want broken up for firewood. After breakfast, I'll take you out to our shed and show you how to do it!"

Bob brightened up.

"I won't be cross, Mums. I love chopping wood! I don't want to be shown, I'll go now."

"No, darling, breakfast is ready, come along. Isn't this a nice cheerful room to live in?"

"It's much nicer than London," said Babs; "what a pity everybody doesn't live in the country!"

"Then it wouldn't be country any longer," laughed her mother.

The old kitchen with its bright fire and big dresser of china on one side, and a glass bookcase of books on the other; with its grandfather clock, and big chintz-covered couch between two casement windows, did indeed look very comfortable this sunny morning. The brightest bit of all was the square oak table with its white cloth, and three happy children sitting up round

27

it ready for their simple breakfast of porridge and bread and butter.

"We'll go out into the woods and get primroses," said Mrs. Percival, "and have bowls of primroses on our window-sills."

"Are we 'lowed to pick them?" questioned Bee.

"Oh yes, you'll see banks of them along the lanes. When we're settled down, we shall have some lovely rambles. There'll be no lessons today. I have too much to do, and if you all help me this morning, we will go out for a walk this afternoon."

About eleven o'clock, Aunt Judy appeared. "You all must come up and have tea with me this afternoon," she said. "I happen to own two or three cows, so I'll send you down milk and butter regularly if you like."

"Thank you very much," said Mrs. Percival.

"Aunt Judy, may we see your cows when we come?" asked Babs. "We want to see all the animals we can, and get to know them. We don't know much about cows and sheep, do they have names?"

"My cows do. Nell and Susan and Molly they are called. If you're fond of animals I can show you quite a few, for I spend most of my time amongst them. I have a lot of moor ponies, but you won't see them this afternoon."

28

The children looked at their aunt with shining eyes. To have ponies seemed to them the height of bliss.

"I cannot understand where you are," said Mrs. Percival. "When I knew you, of course you were at the Hall."

"Yes, but I left a year later when John married, and took over the Dower House, known to the natives as High Clover. I went in for breeding Dartmoor ponies, but now-a-days I keep them for the amusement I get out of them. Do your children ride?"

"Oh no, what chance have they had?"

"But we could," said Bob eagerly, "we could stick on anything. I know I could!"

"Ah well," said his aunt; "we'll see what can be done."

Then Miss Percival departed, Bob politely holding open the gate for her.

CHAPTER THREE

COUSIN HARRY

B EE danced round the room.

"Mums!" she cried, "going out to tea!"

"And ponies!" cried Bob; " 'sposing Aunt Judy lets us ride one?"

It was difficult for them to keep still; they were so excited, so Mrs. Percival suddenly thought of several things she wanted from the village shop, and told them they might find their way there and shop for her.

"You will just have time before dinner. I will give you a list of what I want. I will give some money to Babs to pay for what you get, Bee can take care of the list and Bob must carry the basket. Go straight there and back, for you will have no time to dawdle."

The children got into their coats and went off across the bridge, and up the lane to the village. Everything they saw interested them. They met a man driving some pigs, they saw some budding primroses in the bank above the lane, they came to a cluster of white-walled cottages with thatch roofs, they passed a schoolhouse, and heard the children's voices inside it, then they came to the post office and general store. The door was open, a fat woman leaning her elbows on the counter was talking to her customer, an old man with a long white beard.

"We've all come to shop for Mums," Babs said importantly.

"Ay my pretties, ye'll be down to Ferry House, an' I be pretty zafe tu 'ave what you've come arter!"

Sure enough she had, but whilst she was packing the basket, she talked in such broad Devonshire that the children could not understand her.

The children were turned into the garden till four o'clock, when they were to come in and make themselves tidy for the tea-party. And this time their mother gave them garden jobs to do. At the back of the house was a small vegetable plot, but it was overgrown with weeds, and weeding, as their mother reminded them, was what they could do quite as well as anyone else.

They talked more than they worked, they stopped to hear and look at a lark soaring up into the blue sky above them; they peeped over the hedge when some cows went by driven by a boy no bigger than Bee, and then they heard the sound of voices, and looking over the hedge again, they saw a small boy riding a white pony accompanied by a gentleman.

The little boy sat his pony in a very easy assured way. He was coming down the lane from the village, and stopped his steed upon the bridge.

"There, Mr. Dennison," they heard him cry out, "there's a monstrous fish! Look at him!"

"What a nice boy," said Babs.

He did look a nice boy, though there was something in the way which he held himself that Bob did not like. He had dark brown hair, a rosy face, and was dressed in a brown riding suit with gaiters to match.

"He thinks an awful lot of himself," Bob muttered.

"I like his brown velvet cap," whispered Bee.

The riders came on; they were going up the lane to the moor. As they passed the cottage the boy looked up and caught sight of the three heads over the hedge. They bobbed out of sight at once. But they heard him laugh and say something to the gentleman with him, which they could not catch.

"I'd like to know him," said Babs, as they went on with their weeding.

Bob heaved a sigh.

"I'd like to be him riding a pony 'stead of this old weeding."

"It will soon be time to go indoors," said Babs consolingly, "and Mums says we mustn't wish to be other people, because we wouldn't fit if we were. Our own corner fits us best."

"Shut up, Miss Prig, I wouldn't be in your corner for anything!"

Later, the children walked up the lane towards the moor with their mother. Then, instead of going straight on, they took the first turning to the left, and after walking for about half a mile up another lane with steep banks on either side they came to a big iron gate. This they passed through, and walked up a small neatly-kept drive with shrubberies on each side. They soon came to a low white house with many angles and corners to it. It had originally been a cottage, but had been added to and enlarged from time to time, and now presented a pretty appearance with its latticed windows and flowering creepers over its walls. Close to the hall door were some bright flower beds, full of hyacinths and tulips.

The door was opened by an elderly maid, who took them into a very pretty old-fashioned drawing-room full of old china, bright chintzes, and beautiful water-colours on the walls. In another minute, Aunt Judy came in.

"Now then, come along upstairs. This room is only used for grand occasions. I love looking out on the moors."

Up the wide shallow stairs they went, and then at the end of the passage they came into

Miss Percival's sitting-room. It was a charming place. At one end was a big round bay window overlooking the country for miles round. Aunt Judy pointed out the moor to the children.

"I send my ponies out to spend their days there, and they come home in the evening like the cows. I sit at the window, and watch them trotting home."

"Oh, shall we see them today?" cried Bob.

"If your mother lets you stay late enough."

There were plenty of books and flowers in the room, and in another window recess was a round table with a white cloth, upon which was spread a very tempting-looking tea. They were soon sitting round the table enjoying bread and butter and cakes.

Miss Percival and their mother talked together, but the children were rather silent. Bob's thoughts were chiefly on the ponies. Would he be allowed to stroke their noses? Babs was looking round the room with her quick bright eyes. Not a picture or ornament escaped her notice. As for Bee, her whole concentration was upon her tea, she thought of nothing else, and drew a long sigh of regret when she could eat no more. It was a long time since she had had such a sumptuous meal.

Then Aunt Judy produced some big old-fashioned scrapbooks. She and their mother had a lot to say to each other, and the children withdrew to a corner of the room to enjoy their pictures.

Suddenly there was a shout from below: and then clattering feet, and the door burst open:

"Aunt Judy, may I come in?"

"I think you have come in, Harry," said Miss Percival with a laugh.

The children gazed at the newcomer with big eyes. It was the boy they had seen riding up the lane.

"I did not want you here today, Harry, or I would have invited you," said Miss Percival in her frank way; "but as you are here, you can come and shake hands with your aunt, and cousins."

Harry did as he was told. He stared very hard at his strange cousins, and they stared back at him.

"I saw you over the hedge this afternoon," he said; "you couldn't hide, and I knew who you were."

"Look here, Harry, take your cousins into the garden and show them the stables and the animals. I will join you in a few moments."

Harry blithely led the way. When they were downstairs in the garden their tongues moved fast.

"We never knew we had a cousin," said Babs. "Do you live with Aunt Judy?"

"Should think not! My home is the Hall. Haven't you heard of the Hall?"

"No, is it a bit of another house?"

"A bit! Just you come here! Now look over the fields to that big white house in the trees! That's it!"

Pride was in his tone. He stretched himself to his full height.

"It belongs to Dad now. It will all belong to me one day."

"Is your Dad our uncle?" asked Babs.?

"I 'spose he is. Come on, and we'll have the dogs out."

He led the way through a wooden door to a small square yard. There was a black cat washing her face in the sun as she sat on the stable doorstep. Harry opened the stable door, and three rough terriers tumbled out, a mother and two young ones.

Bob had one of the puppies in his arms in a moment, and Babs took hold of the other.

"What darlings! What are they called?"

"The mother is Nancy, the puppies are Rough and Tan. I'll let out Griff. Look out! he may knock you down, but it's only his fun."

Griff was a huge sheep dog; he was young and full of spirits, and the children backed out of his way. The puppies were adorable, but they were a little afraid of Griff.

"I wish we had a dog," said Bob wistfully.

"You should see our dogs," said Harry rather boastfully. "We have a great Dane, and a bulldog, and five or six terriers, and two spaniels, and a collie."

"What do you want such a lot for?" asked Babs, cuddling her puppy.

"We have dozens of everything," said Harry with emphasis.

"Have you any bruvers and sisters?" asked Bee eagerly.

"No, I'm the only one."

"Then you aren't so well off as us," said Bob a little triumphantly. "There are three of us. I s'pose you have to have a lot of dogs to play with, because you've nobody else. We don't want dogs, we have each other."

"Oh, we'd like *one*," cried Babs, "we'll ask Mums if we can have a little puppy."

"I've got a most beautiful nest in a high tree," went on Harry, bent on asserting his superiority; "our carpenter made it for me. It's just like a nest, a huge nest outside, and has cushions in it and it will hold four or five people."

"Do show us it."

"Not today, you can come to tea one day and then I'll show it to you."

Then he took them into the stables, where there were two big brown ponies. Then Aunt

Judy appeared, and Mrs. Percival. They visited the poultry yard, where some white turkeys enchanted the children, and saw the three red-brown cows being driven in from a field to be milked. It was altogether a very happy visit, and on the way home, Bee informed her mother that she had never thought the country could be quite so beautiful as it was.

"I shan't want to go to heaven," she remarked reflectively. "If God lets me live here always and for ever, I shall be quite happy."

"Oh no, darling, you will find as you grow older that troubles will come as much in the country as in the town. God never means this earth to be perfect anywhere. He's keeping the best for us by and by!"

"Harry brags!" announced Bob; "he seems to think he's better than us, and he isn't."

"Is he just as naughty, do you think?" asked Mrs. Percival.

"Oh, Bob doesn't mean that," put in Babs eagerly; "Harry keeps talking of all the things he has, and asking us what we've got, and when we say nothing, he looks quite pleased."

"I'll knock him down one day," said Bob aggressively.

"Now look here, children," said their mother; "Harry is your cousin, and you must be friends with him if he wishes you to be. You will be miserable here if you are always quarrelling. He is a lonely little boy, and you must be kind and patient with him. If you don't like some things about him, I am sure there are things about you that he does not like."

The children were silent, then Bee said:

"If he asks us to tea, and lets us climb into his nest, I'll love him!"

"You'd love a crocodile," said Bob scornfully, "or a black beetle. There's nothing you don't say that you love."

"Yes," said Bee complacently. "I loves them all."

CHAPTER FOUR

A RAMBLE ON THE MOOR

THE very next afternoon, when the children were taking a walk with their mother up the lane towards the moor, they met Miss Percival's herd of ponies being driven along by an old man called Joe.

Mrs. Percival stopped him, and while she was speaking to him the children tried to get into touch with the ponies. But these were shy and wild; and such a stampede ensued that Joe had to go on with them, and the children were much disappointed.

"They're such darlings!" said Babs; "such lovely manes and tails! Oh Mums, do you think Aunt Judy would let us ride one of them one day?"

"I don't think they're broken in for riding, dear. They looked to me very wild and untamed."

"Harry rides," said Bob enviously.

They talked a great deal about their cousin, and were not quite certain as to whether they wanted to see him soon again, or not.

Two days later, their Aunt Judy called for Mrs. Percival in her pony trap. She wanted to take her to tea with an old friend some distance off; and after a little hesitation, Mrs. Percival went with her.

The children were happy in the garden, and Fanny would see to them and give them tea.

It was a lovely afternoon. Bob and Babs were trying to build a little house for themselves in the corner of the garden. They had found some old matting in the shed, and some poles; and were tying the poles across from an apple tree to the hedge. It was hard work, and they soon became tired. Bee had perched herself up on a little bit of fencing overlooking the road. She watched the pony trap take her mother off across the bridge and up towards the village, and then announced to her brother and sister that she was going for a walk.

"We'll all go," said Babs; "we'll go up on the moor, and see if we can find those darling ponies."

"Don't make a row, or Fanny will say we mustn't!" advised Bob.

Though they had not been actually forbidden to take a walk, they had an uncomfortable feeling that it might not be allowed. Their mother had gone off in such a hurry, that she had given them no directions as to how they were to spend their afternoon.

41

In a very short time, they were all three pelting along the lane at breathless speed. When they were quite out of sight of their house, they slackened their pace.

"We'll be back in time for tea," said Babs reassuringly.

"Of course we will," echoed Bob.

It seemed a long way to the end of the lane, but they kept steadily on, and at last to their great joy they came to a wooden gate which led straight out on the wide treeless moor.

Sweet smelling golden gorse grew in great clumps upon the short brown turf. Larks were soaring up into the sky singing as they went. There were lovely patches of green rushes, and yellow moss; here and there were dark brown pools in peaty soil. They raced along the little footpaths made by sheep and cattle, they shouted with delight when they frightened two rabbits into their holes; in the distance were a herd of ponies, and these were their goal. When the ponies raised their heads, and saw them coming they trotted away, but the children raced after them, heedless of time or distance. And then at last their legs gave out, and they sat down on the grass to rest.

"Isn't it big and empty here?" said Babs; "no house, nobody, nothing. Only animals; I wonder if they ever lose themselves."

Bob looked round him.

"We have come a long way. Where's the gate in our lane?"

"Over there," pointed Babs, but Bee pointed in the opposite direction. "I'm sure it was that side of us," she insisted.

"We shall never catch up those ponies," said Bob, "I think we'd better be going home."

It was some little time before they began to retrace their steps, for the sun was hot, and they were tired, and Babs was busy plaiting some rushes which she said she would make into a mat.

Bob led the way, and he followed Babs' directions. But after some time they came to some boggy ground, which they had never seen before, so they turned away in another direction, and then found themselves amongst great blocks of granite, and a rushing mountain stream.

This was fascinating; they took off their shoes and stockings and waded in the water, but found it very cold. They dried their feet with their handkerchiefs, and turned their steps in a contrary direction. At last it began to dawn upon them that they had lost their way, and Bob and Babs looked at each other with big serious eyes. Bee began to cry.

"It isn't that I don't like being lost," she

sobbed; "I do, for it's an adventure, but I'm drefully, awfully, tired."

"Well," said Bob sensibly; "Aunt Judy's man Joe always brings the ponies off the moor about tea time—we'll wait till we see them going home, and then we'll follow them."

"But the ponies are out of sight now," objected Babs.

"Look," cried Bob excitedly; "there's somebody moving over there, it's a girl or woman, I see her dress flying in the wind,"

They sprang to their feet, and ran towards the figure in the distance as fast as they could.

They found it was quite a small girl, not much bigger than Babs, and she had a little hand-cart by her side into which she was packing some bits of turf. It was only a rough little box on wheels, but she was getting quite a lot into it.

"I say," Bob called out, "we want to get home, do you know where the Ferry House is?"

She looked up. She was a tidy looking little girl in a big blue overall, and a white worsted cap on a shock of dark brown curls, but her face was thin and white, and she looked tired, and her shoulders were bent like an old woman's.

"You mean Tom Fagan's ole house near Moorcombe, why you be miles out o' your way. You be walkin' straight away from un."

44

"Oh dear!" groaned Babs and Bee together.

"I be goin' that way meself," said the little girl, looking at them with some curiosity; "leastways our cottage lies on road to Moorcombe lane."

"May we come back with you? We don't know the moor very well. You see we've only come to live here lately. We've always been in London."

Bob's tone was very meek.

"What are you doing?" questioned Babs. "Can't you get that earth you're carrying nearer your cottage than this?"

"This be peat, for firin'. 'Tis what Feyther cut back along last summer. Us leaves un tu dry out in sun and wind, and then fetches un when us wants un."

She had packed her small cart, and now, slipping a noose of string round her waist, proceeded to drag it after her along a well-beaten path which the children had not found. Bob at once offered to push the cart along, and as they went their way the little girl began to tell them about herself. She told them that her name was Agnes Dunn, that her father was a labourer on a moor farm about three miles away. She lived in a small cottage with a little brother who was always in bed: his spine was diseased, and he could not sit up at all. Her mother had

45

died a year ago, and she kept house for father and Jimmy.

She soon pointed out the chimneys of the cottage, and in a very short time they came up to it. It was sheltered under a clump of fir-trees.

"Would you like to sit down for a bit and rest?" she asked.

The children were only too willing to do so. They were also curious to see where she lived.

She opened the door and ushered them into a comfortable looking kitchen. There was a peat fire in an open fireplace, and a kettle suspended from a big hook hung over it. The table and dresser with its blue and white plates looked tidy and clean. There was an old-fashioned wooden armchair drawn up to the fire, a wooden form against the wall, a few books in a low book-case, in the corner of the room a small bed with a patchwork quilt over it; and in the bed, with his smooth dark head resting against a pillow, lay Jimmy.

The children looked at him with much interest but with some shyness. Bee was the one who stepped quickly up to him.

"We've heard about you, Jimmy. I'm so sorry you can't get out of bed, but I s'pose you're never tired, and that's a good fing. My legs are quite worn out."

He smiled up into her face.

"I b'ain't tired o' walkin', but o' lyin' still. I sez to Aggie when her be cryin' out along of her back and legs achin', I'd a deal rayther be her than I!"

Agnes produced a chair out of a bedroom that led out of the kitchen, and made Babs sit upon it. Bob took the form, and Bee climbed into the armchair.

"Oh," said Babs looking round her with shining eyes, "I would love to live in a little house like this. Do you dust and sweep and cook all by yourself, Agnes? Do you never have anybody who tells you what to do?"

She shook her head.

"Feyther helps me when he be tu home. But he be off early in the morning, and takes his vittles wi' him. An' Jimmy be left long hours to hisself, for I be not through school yet. Only Teycher, her be good at lettin' me home early."

"And can you cook dinners and puddings and cakes?" questioned Babs with awe. "Who taught you?"

"I larned meself afore Mother were took tu horsepital."

"Do you do everyfing?" asked Bee looking out of the window and seeing some fluttering white garments on a line. "Do you wash clothes, and scrub and dust and sweep and light fires, and clean the silver?"

47

Agnes nodded importantly, and then she gave
a little sigh; "But I do ache at times, 'tis awful
work gettin' up so early for Feyther's meal."

"What time do you get up?"

"Five o'clock now."

The children gazed at her in admiration. She
looked so small to be doing a woman's work in
addition to her schooling! A wave of enthusiasm
rushed over Babs' soul.

"Oh, if only I had a little house of my own,
I could do it, I know I could do it, and no one
over me, or to tell me what to do!"

Her rapt expression made Bob laugh.

"*You!*" he said scornfully; "you can't make
your own bed properly. Fanny says you're more
trouble than you're worth!"

Bee was now approaching Jimmy's bed again.
She was greatly interested in him. She smiled at
him in a friendly fashion, then suddenly said:

"Can you play cat's cradle? Mother taught
me when I was in bed with measles."

"I can read," said Jimmy, looking at her with
earnest pathetic brown eyes. "I loves readin';
but I can't get hold of no books, and I've read
Aggie's, even her old spellin' book I reads for
somethin' to do."

"Oh, I'll bring you lots and lots and lots of
books," Bee promised eagerly. "We have heaps
of them."

48

"If we don't get home soon, it will be dark," said Bob, getting up from his seat wearily; "and Mums will wonder where we are. We'll come and see you another day."

They said good-bye to their new friends, and Agnes came to the door, and pointed out to them the path that they must take.

"I goes tu school every day your way," she said, "and I knows the Ferry House well."

"Then," suggested Babs, "come in tomorrow and we'll give you a story book for Jimmy."

Agnes looked pleased. They wished each other good-bye, and then Bob and Babs started at a brisk pace towards home, Bee following them with lagging steps. It was a very weary little trio that reached home nearly an hour later, and Mrs. Percival met them at the door with an anxious face. It was long past tea-time, and Fanny had been scouring the village for them, and had just returned to the house very tired and very cross.

"It wasn't right of you to go off like that; I cannot have you taking long walks over the moor by yourselves," said their mother. "You must not do it again. Now come to tea at once. No, I don't wish to hear anything about your wanderings till you have had your tea. You have given both Fanny and myself a great deal of trouble and anxiety."

Mrs. Percival seated them at the table, gave them their tea and left them alone, a sign that she was not pleased with them.

Later on, she heard all about Agnes and Jimmy, and was quite willing that they should lend Jimmy some of their story-books.

"Oh Mums," cried Babs, "I wish, I wish I could be Agnes. Fancy having a house to manage all by herself; and she's no older than I am. It must be perfectly lovely having it all to do by yourself, and no grown-up person to interfere!"

Mrs. Percival looked at her eldest daughter with rather a sad little smile.

"And this is the Babs who hates dusting her bed-room, or helping Fanny to make the beds!"

"But that's because it's just helping; if nobody could do it but me, it would be quite, quite different!"

Babs was rather discontented and cross for the next few days. Agnes arrived one day, and Mrs. Percival talked with her, and sent her home with not only some story-books for Jimmy, but with some cake, and a promise that they would all come over and see Jimmy soon on a fine afternoon.

Then one morning Mrs. Percival said to Babs:

"Now, Babs, you will have an opportunity of proving how useful you can be in a house.

50

Fanny is going away for a holiday. She has a
brother at Newton. He has just come there, and
I'm going to let her have two days' holiday.
You will be able to help me a great deal."

"Oh Mums!"

Babs did not look very pleased.

"Well, I thought you were longing to cook
and scrub and dust."

"Oh, but that was all by myself."

Then Mrs. Percival had a bright idea. She
did not say anything more just then, but waited
till the day came for Fanny to leave. She never
asked Babs to help her in any way that day,
but the next morning before breakfast she
called the children to her room.

To their extreme surprise they found their
mother in bed.

"I am sorry, darlings," she said. "I am very
tired and I thought I would take the opportunity
of having a thorough good rest. So I mean to
stay in bed all day. I am quite sure that you,
Babs, will be able to manage the house by yourself. Your chance has come, you see, and I
know that Bob and Bee will help you all they
can."

The children gazed at their mother with big
eyes.

Then Babs rose to the occasion. Surely, as
her mother had said, this would be her oppor-

tunity. She would be able to fill Fanny's place perfectly, and her mother would discover what a treasure she had in her eldest daughter.

She drew herself up with considerable importance as she walked out of the room.

"I will bring you your breakfast very soon, Mums," she said; "I shall find everything quite easy."

But in her heart as she walked downstairs and found no fire in the kitchen, and all the windows shuttered, and the crumbs and dust on the dining-room carpet, and no boiling kettles or any hot water, she began to feel that she had a good deal of work before her.

CHAPTER FIVE

BABS AS HOUSEKEEPER

"ISN'T this fun?" cried Bob, capering up and down in the kitchen. "We can have exactly what we like for breakfast. I'm going to the larder to have a look round. Bee and me will lay the breakfast."

"You must help me light the fire," said Babs sharply; "and Mums must have her breakfast first."

"You needn't order me what I'm to do. I shall do what I like, but I'll help you light the fire!"

Coals, and wood, and paper, were stuffed into the fire over the dead ashes. There was no draught, so the fire would not burn, and Babs grew very cross and impatient. At last they emptied the grate properly, and after about half-an-hour's delay the fire began to burn. But Babs had burnt one of her fingers, and Bob's hand and face were as black as a sweep's. Bee had disappeared. She was at the garden gate having an animated conversation with the milk boy.

It seemed now as if one misfortune happened

53

after another; Bee carrying the milk into the house tripped over a stone, and let the jug fall from her hands. In a moment the milk was spilt over the gravel path and the jug broken. She had to go to the village to fetch some more. Bob tried his hand at cleaning the doorstep, but he could not make it look as Fanny did, and carrying his pail of water through the hall upset it at the dining-room door, and the water flowed over the carpet there, leaving a dark muddy stain. Babs tried to fry some bacon. She burnt one lot, and then boiled some eggs. At ten o'clock Mrs. Percival received her breakfast. A cup of half cold tea, with a good deal spilt upon the tray, some blackened toast, and a very hard boiled egg, was what was brought to her by Babs, who looked hot and dirty, and with difficulty could speak cheerfully.

"Bob won't sweep the carpet, and Bee is playing in the garden."

"Never mind, dear. I expect you will do better alone. Have your breakfast and then you can go straight on. There's cold meat in the larder, and we can have a rice pudding for dinner. You will find some potatoes in the larder. But you won't forget to make your beds, and tidy your bed-rooms."

Babs crept downstairs with a forlorn feeling in her heart.

How could she do it all? How did Agnes manage? And why was their house so dusty and dirty compared with hers? Bob and Bee were quite willing to come to breakfast. Bob got hold of some cake, and that with plenty of jam on his bread and butter contented him. The next hour or two seemed one long nightmare to Babs. She cut her finger trying to peel the potatoes, she spilt a saucepan of water over the fire and nearly put it out, she broke two dishes and a plate. They slipped from her hand as she was washing up. And at twelve o'clock, when she felt hopeless and helpless, who should appear at the door but their cousin Harry! He looked rosy, clean, and smiling, and when he saw the general untidiness and muddle in the house he said:

"Hullo, what's up?"

"We're playing at housekeeping," said Bob, who was trying to clean a pair of boots, "like to come and help us? Fanny is out and Mums is in bed."

Harry thought it would be rather fine.

"I'll make a pudding!" he said, "if you'll give me the sugar and currants."

So Bob, delighted with the idea, led him off to the kitchen cupboard, and Babs, feeling quite in despair about everything, left them together, and went up to tidy the bed-rooms.

Would the morning never come to an end? Then in a short time she heard shrieks from the kitchen, and going down found Harry and Bob pelting each other with lumps of dough, and chasing each other round the table. The pudding had been made in a fashion, and then they had come to words. Harry had called Bob a dumpling and Bob had called him a suet-faced idiot. Then Harry had hit him in the face with a piece of his dough, and that started the battle: the pudding was pulled to pieces, for the purpose of pelting each other. Though they were laughing, there was an angry light in Bob's eyes, and a spiteful twist about Harry's lips.

"Go away, Harry!" cried Babs. "You've only made things worse. Stop it, Bob!"

But neither would stop, and at last they rushed out of the kitchen, and in a few minutes fists were being used in real earnest.

Bee came running in.

"They're fighting, Babs, and Harry's nose is bleeding!"

Babs sat down on the floor and burst into tears.

"I've looked in the oven and the rice pudding is burnt to cinders," she sobbed; "and the water is dried up in the potato saucepan and they're burnt too. Everything has gone wrong, and I don't care if the boys kill each other. I shan't go near them!"

Bee looked at her sister with surprise. She herself cried very easily, but Babs hardly ever cried, and scorned everyone who did.

"I fink I'll go up to Mums," Bee murmured, edging towards the door; but Babs sprang up and stopped her.

"You aren't to go up to Mums telling tales. If you and Bob had helped me properly, everything would have been all right. I can't do it all."

But at this juncture the door opened, and in walked Mrs. Percival.

"I thought my poor Babs would have had enough of it by this time," she said, drawing her tearful dishevelled little daughter into her arms. "My darling, I wanted you to see that keeping a house clean and tidy, and cooking, was not so easy as you thought it. I am rested now, and we shall soon get order out of this confusion."

In a very short time Mrs. Percival had done wonders, and then Bob came creeping into the house, with a black eye and a swollen lip. He looked ashamed of himself when he was confronted by his mother.

"Harry's gone home," he said in answer to his mother's enquiries. "We didn't mean to fight. We began it in fun, but then he really hurt me, and he tried to, so I gave it to him

57

back again. His tutor came after him, and stopped us. I was getting the best of it."

"Go upstairs, and bathe your face," his mother said quietly. "I am too busy to attend to you just now, but I am ashamed that you should fight with your cousin about nothing at all."

They had a very simple dinner that day. Just cold meat and bread and cheese, but Babs was very humbled by her experience, and never again wanted to manage a house alone with no one to help or interfere with her. They did not see Harry for some days. His father and mother had returned home, and Bob felt a little uncomfortable when he saw them in church on Sunday. Had Harry told them of the fight, he wondered? His conscience told him that he had been the first to use his fists.

A note from Aunt Judy on Monday morning put all thoughts of Harry out of their heads, for this was what she wrote:

"My dear nephew and nieces,

I have now three rough little scamps of ponies warranted safe for riding. Would you like to come up to my paddock to-morrow afternoon, and show me what kind of riders you are? For if you can keep your seats, and promise to treat them kindly,

58

Dan, Ran and Chumps shall be yours. Tell your mother I will stable them up here, and they will run in my paddock by day. You will be able to come and get them when you want them. And old Joe will be willing to take you about on the moor.

Your affectionate Aunt Judy."

There were screams of delight from the children when the letter was read. Mrs. Percival smiled, and shook her head rather doubtfully.

"I don't know whether Bee is not too small for a pony. I shall be afraid for all of you. Dartmoor ponies are sometimes very tricky!"

When Tuesday came, the children with their mother arrived at their aunt's at half-past-two in the afternoon.

Aunt Judy had not only had the three ponies brushed and smartened up, but on their backs were three new saddles.

All the children acquitted themselves well. Perhaps of the three Babs was the most nervous. Bee sat her pony as if to the manner born, and Bob's one hope was to have a gallop. He was given Ran, a chestnut; Babs had Dan, who was a mouse colour; and Bee had Chumps, with a black coat, and very gentle eyes.

Old Joe walked and trotted them up and down, and round the paddock, and Aunt Judy

59

carried their mother off to the house to have a quiet chat with her in her pretty upstairs sitting-room, from which they had a full view of the young riders in the paddock.

Half an hour later, Mrs. Percival came out into the paddock to call her children indoors.

"Your uncle is here with Harry, and would like to see you."

The children left their ponies with great reluctance, but Joe told them that they had had quite enough riding for the first day.

They followed their mother into their aunt's drawing-room, where their Uncle Ralph was standing on the hearthrug. He looked tall and grave, but shook hands with each of them in turn.

"You have made friends with Harry," he said, "and your mother I hope has made friends with me at last. Is this Bob? About Harry's age, eh? Well, I think the arrangement I want to make is a good one."

He was speaking more to their mother than to them.

"I must think about it," she said very quietly.

"What is Uncle Ralph's arrangement Mums?" Bob asked, as they went home. "Is it anything about me?"

"He wants you to go up to the Hall every day, and do lessons with Harry and his tutor."

"Oh, Mums, that would be jolly! Better than learning with girls."

"Mayn't we go too?" asked Babs.

"No, you will still do lessons with me. Now that we are settling down, we must start lessons again."

The children felt rather sobered. They had forgotten all about lessons, and none of them were fond of learning.

Bob was the only one who viewed the future with joy.

"I think," he informed his mother that night, "that Harry wants another boy with him. When he brags of all he has, I mean to knock him down. He'll soon stop it. I think he's a little afraid of me. He got the worst of it the other day."

"I shall be ashamed of my son if he tries to fight and bully on every occasion."

"Harry isn't very nice, Mums. He likes to talk to us, but he's a boaster."

"I want you to be friends with Harry," said his mother, speaking very earnestly.

"I do like him, Mums. I'll try to be kind to him, but he seems as if he thinks he's better than we are."

In another week, Bob was going every morning to the Hall from nine till one. The little girls did their lessons at home with their mother, but in the afternoons they would often ride over the moor with their ponies, or take walks with their mother and explore the country lanes and woods. And one day they paid another visit to Agnes and her brother.

They found Agnes at home; the cottage was still the picture of neatness and cleanliness, and Jimmy smiled in a very friendly way at all of them. While Mrs. Percival was talking to Agnes, Bee slipped across to Jimmy's bed.

"Did you read the books we sent you by Agnes?"

"All of 'un! I did true enough, and liked 'un fine."

"Will you *never* get out of bed all your life?" Bee asked, her blue eyes full of pity as she gazed upon Jimmy's thin wasted little figure.

"Doctor says not, but I ain't goin' to have a long life. I heard un tell feyther so."

"Oh, Jimmy, does that mean you'll die? Aren't you 'fraid?"

" 'Fraid o' what? I ain't afraid o' God. Agnes have a Sunday School taycher—her comes tu me an' learns I about God. He be my Feyther, an' Jesus He be my Saviour, and They both on 'un loves me proper! Bettern Feyther do! I ain't 'fraid to go to They!"

Bee stared at him.

"I didn't fink you were a good boy."

"I ain't."

There was silence, then Jimmy bent his head forward and spoke in a confidential tone:

"Tell'ee what I lies thinkin' on, an' can't get the rights of un nohow. What be 'eaven like? Some folks say un be a gert town wi' streets o' gold, and jool gates; an' others say un be a garden wi' fruit an' trees an' rivers. I'd dearly like to be sure of where I be goin'."

Bee's eyes were big with bewilderment.

"I don't often fink of heaven," she confessed; "but then I'm not going there so soon as you are. I'll find out, Jimmy, and tell you. Grown-up people will be sure to know."

The very next day after this, they all went to the Hall to tea. There were quite a lot of people in the big drawing-room when they got there, for there were several visitors staying in the house. Bob and Babs went off with Harry to see a squirrel he had, but Bee was talking to her uncle, and presently in one of those pauses that sometimes occur, Bee's clear little voice rang through the room.

"Please will you tell me egsackly what heaven's like. You're sure to know, and I've got to find out."

"That's a poser," murmured a young man, looking at his host with twinkling eyes.

The hum of conversation was resumed. Bee's uncle looked at her with astonishment.

"I haven't the faintest notion," he said; "nor more has anyone, I believe. Why on earth does a small child like you want to know about heaven?"

"It's for a boy going there. I told him I'd find out."

She had been sitting on her uncle's knee; now he was called away, and he put her down. The young man near took hold of Bee's hand and pulled her towards him.

"Come and speak to me, you young theologian! Your uncle Ralph is my first cousin, so we must be related too. You can call me Cousin Ted if you like."

Bee looked at him with friendly eyes.

"I wonder," she said in a confidential whisper, "if you know more than Uncle Ralph. I should like to know what heaven is like."

"Ah, you want to know too much! But one day if you come and see me in my house the other side of the moor, I'll get my old nurse to talk to you. She's my housekeeper now, but she used to tell me a lot about heaven, when I was a boy."

"How soon could I come?" asked Bee eagerly.

"Just as soon as you like, only we must ask your mother about it."

"Only me, or Babs and Bob too?"

Her mother called Bee just then, for Babs

and Bob had come back, and she was leaving.

"Who is Ted, Mums?" asked Bee as she walked home hand in hand with her mother.

"He's a young cousin of your dear father's. He was a soldier, but was badly wounded in the War, and he became a doctor afterwards. He has a country practice not far from here. He is obliged to have an outdoor life because of his health."

"I love him," said Bee simply.

Babs and Bob giggled.

"He's a friend of *mine*!" she said. "He doesn't know you, and doesn't want to, only *me*."

"Bee, darling, if you have a large heart for loving, remember those at home must come first."

Bee did not answer. She knew what her mother meant, and her momentary anger died away.

But when she went to bed that night she said in a very firm tone to herself:

"I'll go to his house, as soon as ever I can!"

CHAPTER SIX

BEE AND HER PONY

IT was some days before Bee could carry out her resolve. And then one afternoon Harry came round on his pony and asked the three of them to ride out with him on the moor. Mrs. Percival hesitated:

"By yourselves? Without Joe, or your tutor?"

"But we can ride like anything now," exclaimed Babs; "Joe says we've nothing more to learn—only to practise."

"And the moor is flat, and we won't go among the rocks," said Harry.

So with a little more persuasion Mrs. Percival yielded.

They ran up the lane to get their ponies, and twenty minutes later were riding up towards the moor, all talking and laughing at the top of their voices. Two of Harry's terriers accompanied them. It was a lovely afternoon in the beginning of July.

Harry knew his way about the moor thoroughly. He took his cousins between two great Tors, and then along a green level valley, and it was

66

here that Bee suddenly put a question to Harry.

"Where does that doctor cousin of yours live? Somewhere on the moor, he said."

"Yes," said Harry pointing with his riding crop over a Tor in the distance. "It's the other side of Bell Beacon. You mean Cousin Ted, don't you?"

Bee nodded. The spirit of adventure seized her. She would ride off by herself, and go and see that old nurse who could talk about heaven. But she waited till Harry called a halt. He had brought some cakes and fruit with him. Dismounting, they let the ponies graze by the side of a rippling stream. It was very pleasant lying on the short sunny turf. Babs began to pick some whortleberries, and then very quietly Bee glided away round the corner behind some hillocks. Chumps leisurely followed her. There was perfect understanding between Chumps and his little mistress. Now she turned, and in a moment was on his back.

"Chumps, we're going to the other side of Bell Beacon."

Away Chumps trotted, the path was level and not too stony, and for some time Bee rode happily on. A little thrill passed through her. This was an adventure after her own heart. She could ride about the moor as well as Harry, though he had had a pony for years, and she had only had hers for two months. She had ridden about two miles when suddenly she came upon a herd of moor ponies. A whinny from them made Chumps throw up his head. He recognized some of his old friends, and with an answering neigh he simply bolted in their direction.

They fled, and he chased them, and Chumps was so excited that he quite forgot his young rider. His one desire was to get with his friends again. In vain Bee tugged at his bit, he got it between his teeth and overtook the herd. Then as he dashed over a hummock, Bee lost her balance and fell over his head. For one moment she did not know where she was. Happily her resting place was a soft thick bed of heather, and when she picked herself up, she felt none the worse for her tumble. But Chumps had disappeared. In the distance she saw the herd, and knew that he was among them. It was a disaster that she had not expected, and sitting down among the heather again, she began to cry. This adventure of hers was turning out all wrong. Of course, she ought to catch her pony, but he was almost out of sight, and what chance was there of getting to Cousin Ted's?

She cried until she could cry no more. There was nobody near her to dry her tears, or comfort her. And then courage came back to her. If she couldn't catch her pony, she must get back to the others.

She set off at a trot which soon changed into a walk. What a long way she must have come! And how hot the sun was!

"P'raps somebody will come along," she told herself. "Agnes did. I wish they'd be quick and do it."

Nobody seemed in sight. And then away in the distance she saw a car. Bee was not stupid. She knew at once that her best chance was to get to the road, and so she waded valiantly through the heather and over the rocks and stones till she reached the main road. Two cars flashed by her, taking no notice of her waving to them.

"They won't stop! Horrid things!" she cried, tears again springing to her eyes, and then a cart and shaggy pony came up. An old un- shaven man, surrounded by pots and pans, both new and old, was the driver.

"Oh stop! Stop!" cried Bee dancing up and down in a frenzy of excitement. "I want to be tooken up and nobody will do it!"

"Hey now!" said the old man pulling up his pony and looking at her with surprise, "an' what may be ye doin', li'l' maid, out here?"

"I'm partly lost, and partly left behind by my pony," she said. "And I eiver want to go home or to Cousin Ted's house."

"An' where be that tu, li'l' maid?" enquired the old man; "an' who be Cousin Ted?"

"He's a doctor and he lives near Bell Beacon. Do you know him?"

The old man took off his hat, and wiped his forehead with a dirty red handkerchief, and then he regarded Bee with gravity.

"A reckon 'tis young Doctor Perciwal you'm manin'! I were in his house a couple hours back along."

"Yes," said Bee, hope dawning in her wet blue eyes, "that's him. Oh, do let me sit up in the cart with you, while you take me to him."

She was already clambering in, thankful to have met with somebody who could take care of her.

"Tis out o' my way sure enough," muttered the old man, "but her be a wee maid out here by her loneself!"

He turned his cart round, and began to jog back along the road by which he came. Bee recovered her spirits. She told him all about herself, and asked him unanswerable questions about himself. James Tolly was his name and he was a travelling tinker.

"Are you a good old man?" Bee asked. "I wonder if you can tell me anything about heaven? I'm out this way because of that. I've got to find out for a boy who's going there."

The old man looked at her.

"Ay, li'l' maid, a 'ave a good missis up there, alang wi' a purty li'l' maid o' me awn. 'Tis where us orl be journeyin' sure enough. A sits in chapel an hears tell on 'em."

"What's it like? Is it country or town? Is it one big golden Palace with inside rooms, or is it fields of beautiful flowers? Do tell me all you can."

Bee lifted an eager sparkling face to the old tinker. He looked down at her with a broad smile upon his brown wrinkled face. Then holding the reins in one hand he put the other into his coat pocket, and pulled out a shabby brown book.

"This 'ere story be written by one o' me own trade, Bunyan by name. I be fair taken wi' the buke, an' the 'count o' t'other side be winderfall! Winderfall!"

He twisted the reins round one arm, and the shaggy pony stopped, only too glad to have a munch at the grass on the edge of the road. Then he began to read to Bee from the *Pilgrim's Progress*.

"You are going now, said the shining angels to Christian, to the Paradise of God wherein you shall see the tree of Life and eat of the never fading fruits thereof, and when you come there you shall have white robes given you and your walk and talk shall be every day with the King, even all the days of eternity."

71

"Go on," cried Bee as the tinker paused. He read on a page or two, and though there was much that Bee did not understand, she loved the sound of it all, especially the description of the crowns, the harps, and the bells in the City ringing for joy.

"Well, li'l' maid, du ee fancy un?"

"Oh, I like hearing it."

James Tolly put the book in his pocket again and they jogged along.

"I s'pose," Bee said thoughtfully, "that heaven is somefing like our world here, some of it is a town, and some of it country. Would a cripple boy have the bells rung for joy when he arrived over the river, do you think? I'd like to tell Jimmy 'bout it."

"For sure 'ee would."

Bee looked up into the blue sky above her, a smile upon her lips.

"I do so wish," she said earnestly, "that I could get up in the sky just high enough to see the gates."

She was brought down to earth rather quickly by a voice from a passing car hailing her. It was Cousin Ted himself.

"Oh," she cried, "I'm coming to see you, and your old nurse. You told me I could and I'm on my way."

The young doctor was rather taken aback.

But Bee was quickly transferred from the cart to the car, old James had some silver pressed into his hand, and then he took his leave, but Bee had some parting words to give him first.

"If you know Agnes and her father who live at Wonnycot, will you tell her brother Jimmy what you read to me?"

"Wonnycot, sure enough I know they. 'Tis a little lass with a sick brother, who minds the house. A'll have a crack wi' un 'bout the golden city next toime a calls. Good-bye, li'l' maid. And thank 'ee kindly, sir."

He turned his pony's head round, and went on his way.

Bee sat up in the car quite excited. She poured out into Cousin Ted's ears the account of her pony running away, and was much disappointed when he said:

"My good child, I can't make off with you like this, when your party will be scouring the moors for you. The sooner I take you home the better."

"But I must be closest to your house," pleaded Bee; "do let me come."

Cousin Ted shook his head.

"Supposing your mother met your pony running wild without you on his back, wouldn't she be anxious?"

Bee had not thought of this.

"But I've taken such a lot of trouble to find

73

you," she cried, "and I must be close, and I fought your nurse might give me tea, and it would be an adventure."

"Yes, it must be an adventure for another day though. Now can you tell me the direction you came from? Where are Harry and the others?"

Bee looked wildly round the moor, and could not tell.

"I've forgotten all about them," she said indifferently.

Dr. Percival set his car going in the direction of Bee's home, and on the way back he remonstrated with her for her want of thought.

"You youngsters run amok, with no thought of the trouble you give your belongings. Now you shall come to tea with me properly one day next week if your mother will let you."

"All of us?" asked Bee with a serious air.

"All of you if you like."

"I'd like to be alone best," she said, "Babs always talks me down."

"Oh there'll be a chance for each of you," said the young doctor laughing.

His car got over the ground swiftly. And then as they were leaving the moor they suddenly came upon Harry and Bob and Babs.

They were hurrying home to tell Mrs. Percival that they had lost Bee, and very much relieved they were when they saw her. Harry was cross.

"I shan't take you kids out again," he said; "you've spoilt my afternoon's sport, all this search and fuss over Bee!"

"I'm glad she'll be home before her mother is made anxious," said Cousin Ted. He drove his car on, and stayed to tea at the Ferry House. They were all anxious over Chumps, but when Aunt Judy heard about it, she said, "Oh he'll come over tonight with the rest of my ponies."

And that is what he did do, trotting in the middle of them with his bridle and saddle and looking quite pleased at his exploit.

When Bee went to bed, her mother had a long talk with her, but it was some time before Mrs. Percival understood the reason of her little daughter's action.

"And don't you think Mums might have told you about heaven?"

Bee wriggled in bed.

"Babs and Bob always laugh," she said, "I like to do my fings private from them!"

"Well, darling, you can ask as many people as you like about heaven, but remember if you want to go there you must do the right thing, not the wrong. It was going against my wishes to go off by yourself, and you might have been left out on the moor all night. If I had seen Chumps come home without you, what should I have thought?"

Bee hung her head.

"Would you have liked poor Mums to be so anxious and frightened about you?" asked Mrs. Percival.

"No—oo," said Bee, then she added with one of her funny little spurts of truthfulness:

"But I should have loved the fuss of being lost and found, and being kissed and cried over when I did come back! And it would have been an adventure—and if I hadn't gone off by myself I shouldn't have met Mr. Tolly, and—and I loves him with all my heart!"

"Your mother comes last in your thoughts. Good-night, Bee."

"I loves you always the best, darling Mums. I reely didn't fink you'd be sorry and anxious, and I'll never go off alone again, never never, and I'm sorry I did it."

CHAPTER SEVEN

COUSIN TED'S STORY

COUSIN TED did not forget to give his invitation for tea. He came for the children one afternoon at three o'clock. They were ready and waiting for him. It was a very hot breathless day with a thick hazy blue sky overhead. Bob and Babs chattered away to their new cousin. Bee was very quiet, though her thoughts were busy. When they were out on the moor, her eyes scanned every road before them.

Cousin Ted noticed that she was looking about rather anxiously, and asked her the reason for it.

"I'm hoping to see Mr. Tolly," she said, "he goes round and round the moor mending pots and pans and selling kettles."

"Yes, I know him, but he's left this part for the present. He gives us a call about once a month."

"I hope I shall see him again," said Bee.

"Bee is so ridiculous," said Babs; "she keeps a book with a list of her 'friends' as she calls them, and her last one is 'James Tolly the Tinker'. She told Mums she loves him! Just fancy that!"

77

"You've been looking in my book," said Bee angrily; "mean spy-cat!"

"James Tolly's my friend too, Bee. We think a lot of James. He's a local preacher," said Cousin Ted.

"I'd like to go round the moor with him," said Bob stoutly, "it must be fun going to all the farms and houses and selling things."

They soon arrived at a little moorland village with a church, a school, a post office and a cluster of cottages. Cousin Ted lived at one end of it. His house was reached through a white gate and a short drive. It was a low old-fashioned cottage with thatched roof, and casement windows. Babs and Bee fell in love with it at once.

He opened a glass door which led into a small square hall. There was a curious picture over an old-fashioned fireplace. The children gazed at it admiringly. A big man was wading through a very rough river, with a tiny child upon his shoulders. He was staggering under the child's weight, which seemed strange. The water was seething and dashing round him, and it was very dark. Only a strange light that seemed to surround the child, lightened up the picture.

"Who's the man?" asked Bee.

"St. Christopher. Ever heard of him? I'll tell you the story by and by. Now then, this is Mrs.

Comfort. She's my nurse and the comfort of my life, I can tell you."

A very stout smiling-faced woman had appeared before them.

"Three hungry young visitors, Comfy—and a very hungry man. Shall we come into the dining-room at once?"

"Ay, sir, I'll have the tea made in a moment, and there be hot cakes in the oven. Bless the pretty darlings! All of a size too! Which be which, now?"

Babs drew herself up importantly:

"I'm the eldest, and my name is Babs. Bob comes next me, and Bee is the littlest one."

"A bunch of bees!" said Mrs. Comfort, and then she bustled away, and they found themselves in a long low dining-room with a great black beam across the ceiling. A square table was laid with a white cloth, and Bee thought the tea service was one of the prettiest she ever had seen. All the cups and saucers were a dark rose colour, with a tiny bunch of flowers in the middle of them. There were buns and biscuits and cakes, and honey and jam upon the table. Mrs. Comfort evidently remembered what children liked for tea. Then she came into the room with a big plate of hot crisp golden tea cakes. Cousin Ted took a big chair at one end of the table, but he made Babs pour out the tea. And then he began to tell them funny stories, and was so comical himself that the children could hardly eat their tea for laughing. It was a merry meal, and when it was over, he took them out into the garden behind the house.

There was a hammock there, and of course the three children must all get into it. Then Mrs. Comfort suddenly appeared.

"Please, sir, you're wanted immediately. 'Tis little Frank Turner, he has scalded his leg terrible his mother says."

"There now! That's the worst of a doctor trying to have a tea-party. It can't be done! Lucky we had the tea, eh? Now you stay here and have a romp. You can't hurt anything in my garden, and you can climb that old oak at the bottom of the lawn if you like. I may not be long. Wait till I come back."

He dashed into the house. Babs and Bob immediately went off to the oak, but Bee lay in the hammock idly, swinging herself to and fro, and thinking. Presently she rolled out of it, and trotted into the house. She pushed open a door, and found Mrs. Comfort in the kitchen having her own tea. A tabby cat was on her knee. She welcomed Bee heartily.

"Please, Mrs. Comfy, will you tell me what heaven is like? Cousin Ted said you would. Mr. Tolly read me a little about it, but I'd like you

80

to tell me too. I'm not going there myself just yet, but I fink a boy that I know is going soon, and o' course he'd like to know about it."

"Tell you about heaven, lovey? Ay, that I will, all that I knows from the good Old Book. What a happy little boy to be going there soon! I'd like to be told that I was."

"Would you? But you have to die first."

"Well, that be but a little door, into a great glory. Heaven, dearie! I sit and I sigh for it at times. No dust or dirt or stairs and steps for achin' feet, no aches or pains at all, no bad sight or failin' breath, no tears, no disappointments, no sin to come between our Lovin' Father and oursels. The Father's House, and us wi' Him. An' the rest after all our toil, and the peace after all the fightings and noise o' life!"

"Yes," said Bee, her blue eyes fixed anxiously upon Mrs. Comfort, "but Jimmy would like to run about and play. He hasn't been able to do that, you know. Mr. Tolly read about music and bells. I like that better."

"Well, well, dearie, it seems to me the children will have their part in the Father's House, just as they do down here; their rooms will be different to the old and tired and disappointed ones. There'll be no lack of song, and music, harps going it says; and we're told the children shall play together in the streets."

81

"And shall we have story-books up there and games?"

"You'll have all you want, and you can't want more," said Mrs. Comfort sagely. "Tell your little friend of the beautiful flowers and fruit he will see, and the white-robed throng of little children already there, and above all the Loving Saviour who says His Kingdom is filled with His little ones."

"Go on," said Bee breathlessly; "tell me more."

Mrs. Comfort repeated slowly:

" 'And God shall wipe away all tears from their eyes, and there shall be no more death, neither sorrow nor crying, neither shall there be any more pain.' That's what the Book tells us, dearie, and so we know that there'll be nothing in heaven to make us unhappy."

"I'd like to go there," said Bee wistfully; then she added quickly: "Thank you, Mrs. Comfort, I'll tell Jimmy all I can remember. I s'pose a lot of the people arrive there crying, and then God wipes their tears away. It sounds nice, doesn't it? What's your cat's name?"

With a child's quick change of thought Bee now occupied herself with playing with the tabby cat, who was only a big kitten, and was quite willing to jump and prance about after a bit of string. Presently the young doctor returned, and Bee ran out to meet him. They went into the garden, and joined Babs and Bob.

Cousin Ted had brought in with him a lovely basket of strawberries. They all sat down under the lime-tree and ate them. Mrs. Comfort came out with cream and sugar, and while they were enjoying the fruit, Cousin Ted was asked to tell them the story of the big man and little child in the water.

He began at once.

"Once upon a time there lived a very strong man called Offerus. He was so strong that he despised everyone else, and at last said that he wanted to serve only the strongest person on earth. He was told of a very mighty powerful king, whose kingdom was getting bigger every day, and he went off immediately and offered to serve and fight for him. The king took him, and made him his chief armour-bearer, and personal attendant. He went about everywhere with the king and fought for him with great success. One day, the king was angry and swore and used the devil's name in his talk.

" 'Who is the devil?' asked Offerus. 'Is he stronger than you?'

" 'Yes, he is,' replied the king.

" 'Then good-bye,' said Offerus, 'I'll go and serve him. My master must be the strongest in the world.'

83

"So he went off and offered his services to the devil. He did a good many wicked deeds now, and the devil used his strength for his own advantage. One day they were riding out together when they came to a wayside cross. As the devil passed it, he shuddered.

" 'Why do you do that?' asked Offerus.

" 'Because that Cross reminds me of Jesus Christ, and I'm afraid of Him.'

" 'Why? Is He stronger than you are?'

" 'Yes, He is far stronger.'

" 'Good-bye,' said Offerus; 'I shall go and serve Him.'

"So he was led to offer his services to his Lord and Saviour, and he was ready to do the humblest things if by so doing he could please his King. By and by he was told to go to a certain river, and use his great strength in carrying anyone old or feeble across it. He was never to refuse passage to any wayfarer who wanted to be taken across. And then one rough stormy night when the river was in flood, and Offerus was comfortably in his bed, he heard a weak childish voice crying to him from the midst of the storm:

" 'Offerus! Offerus! Take me across the river.'

"Up he got at once, out into the dark night he went, and there on the banks of the swollen river stood a tiny child.

84

"With a kind word to the little mite, Offerus hoisted him on his shoulders, and went down into the black raging water. But he found to his astonishment that he had an intolerable weight upon his back. The frail little child seemed to be bearing him down. He could hardly keep his footing; panting for breath with great drops of sweat upon his brow, Offerus struggled on, every step seemed about to be his last. The waves buffeted him cruelly, his back was bowed and seemed almost broken, his great strength became utterly exhausted and spent.

"And then at last the opposite bank was reached, and he put his passenger down.

" 'Who—what—are you?' he stammered, and then he stared in astonishment. The child had disappeared, and in his stead was a radiant white regal figure standing on the shore.

" 'Offerus, no wonder you sank beneath the weight of your burden. That child was the Christ Child, and can there be a greater weight than the Christ of Heaven and Earth, Who is stronger than the strongest? Offerus, you have not failed your Lord. Henceforth you shall be called 'Christ Offerus', for you have borne the Saviour of the World.' "

The story was over. There was a little silence. Bob broke it.

"What a lovely story! Offerus lived by a river

85

like we do. I should love to carry people over like he did."

"He was a ferry man," said Babs thoughtfully, "though he did it without a boat."

"Let's go and look at the picture again now that we understand it," said Bee.

So they all went back to the house and looked at the picture.

"Is it true, really true?" asked Bee.

"It's the legend of Saint Christopher. That is all I can tell you," said Cousin Ted. "I used to love that story as a boy, and I saw the picture in an old shop in London one day, so I bought it."

Then he turned to Bee.

"Have you got hold of Comfy, and heard all you want?" he asked her. Bee nodded gravely.

"Then I think I must be taking you home. You'll have to ride over to me next time on your ponies."

"We will," cried all the children delightedly.

Mrs. Comfort came to the door to see them off. She kissed Bee on parting, and Bee whispered to her:

"I'll tell Jimmy every bit of what you've told me."

Then the car moved off, and flew over the moor so swiftly that it seemed no time before they were home again. Mrs. Percival was standing at the gate waiting for them, but Bob lingered in the lane looking at the river and the bridge across. The story of Christofferus had taken possession of him.

"I wish," he said, that night when his mother was wishing him good-night; "I wish I was a ferry man!"

"Why, dear?" asked his mother.

"If a storm came and washed the bridge away, I might be one."

"Oh we'll hope that won't happen, Bob. Though I did hear that that bridge was washed away once. It was about three years ago. Why do you want to be a ferry man?"

But Bob could not explain.

He thought in his heart it would be a way of pleasing Jesus Christ if he carried old people and little children across the river. And he determined to learn to swim. Harry could swim, and there was a lake in the grounds of the Hall where the boys were allowed to bathe, but so far he had not made much progress with the swimming lessons which Harry's tutor was giving him.

The very next day he walked down to the river and waded out as far as he could. He found that there was a part of the river that was not so very deep. It really had originally been a ford, but the rushing torrents of water from the moor had made it so uncertain and unsafe that a ferry-boat had been instituted, and later, on, a bridge. Just now owing to a long spell of dry weather the river was very low and Bob found that the water at the deepest part only came up to his armpits. Then he began consulting with Babs, and the result was that in a few days' time the story of Christofferus was being enacted across the river.

Bob put on his bathing suit, and Bee was the first passenger he took across on his back. Babs was the next, but her brother found her rather heavy, and staggered about very unsteadily in the middle of the stream.

Then some girls and boys came down the lane on their way home from school. They thought the game great fun, especially when Bob offered to take two or three of the little ones across. He was successful with several, and then a fat boy about Bob's own age demanded to be taken across. Bob complied with his demand, but in the middle of the stream Jack Woods drummed his heels very sharply against Bob's ribs, causing him to overbalance, and both boys fell.

Jack was up in a moment, but Bob struck his head in falling against a sharp stone, and seemed to have trouble in finding his feet. The next moment, to his sisters' horror, he was being swept down the river by the current into the deep water.

They screamed then, and fled into the house. Mrs. Percival did not take a moment to reach the river, but where was her boy? There was no sign of him. Two little boys were racing along the banks and screaming as they went. She tore after them distractedly, and in another moment to her relief she saw Bob's head just out of the water. He was clinging to the bough of a tree which stretched over the river, but looked as if he could not raise himself.

"Hold on!" his mother called, "help is coming."

Bob looked round at her with strained terrified eyes.

"I can't hold much longer!" he cried. His mother was preparing to plunge in when a hand was laid on her shoulder, she saw a man who had come up with his car on the road behind her.

In an instant his coat was off, and he was in the river. In three minutes' time Bob was landed beside his mother, very wet and very exhausted, and with a nasty cut in his head which had been bleeding freely.

Bob was tucked up in bed, given a hot drink, and his head plastered up. Later on, Mrs. Percival heard the children's story.

She reproved them for their dangerous game.

"Until you can swim, Bob, I shall have to forbid you to have anything to do with the river. You might have been drowned today."

"I should like to be a kind of Christofferus," Bob said.

"There is no occasion for your carrying people across when there's a bridge," said his mother. "You can be like Christofferus in other ways."

"How?"

"In taking service under the strongest King in the World, and in helping all the weak and feeble people that come across your path. It is quite as helpful to carry an old woman's bundle for her, as to carry a traveller over a raging foaming river."

Bob looked uncomfortable. Two days previously he had been walking back from the village with his mother, when they overtook an old woman with a heavy basket of groceries; she lived halfway up the lane above their house, and Mrs. Percival had suggested that Bob should offer to carry it for her.

But Bob had spied Harry and his tutor riding towards them in the distance, and he did not want to do it. He thought that Harry might despise him for carrying an old woman's basket, and as his mother did not insist, he had let the opportunity slip.

Now he said with red cheeks:

"I will try, Mums. I'll carry things for people now whenever I get a chance. I'm very strong— I have much more muscle than Harry. Perhaps I'll grow into a very strong man like Christofferus, I wish I could."

"As long as you use your strength for others, my darling, I shall thank God for giving it to you. But never abuse it by hurting and fighting others."

Bob was silent. Then he took hold of his mother's hand and squeezed it tightly.

"I will take service with the strongest King."

CHAPTER EIGHT

A DARTMOOR GALE

"MUMS, can I speak to you?"
"Yes, dear, what is it?"

Mrs. Percival was busy with her sewing machine in her sitting-room. Both windows were open, and the door, for it was a very hot afternoon. The children were playing out in the garden, and Mrs. Percival longed to be in the fresh air with them, but dresses had to be made, and her clever fingers were hard at work.

Bee looked hot and rather dirty; she had been crouching under a kind of hut made of branches and grass, whilst Bob and Babs had gone out hunting.

"I always stay at home," she had complained, "and you have all the fun."

"You're cooking the dinner," said Babs; "you're the littlest, you can't hunt like we do."

And then when they were out hunting, Bee had crept out of the hut, and found her way into the house.

"Are you tired of playing, Bee?"

"Yes, peoples always finks it's so nice when children play togever. I don't think so, and I'm tired, and I want to talk to you."

"Talk away then. If you're tired, sit down."

Bee deposited herself on the floor at her mother's feet. She always preferred the floor to chairs.

"What do *you* fink heaven is like, Mums? I've asked lots o' people, and you said I could go and see Jimmy tomorrow, and I want to be quite sure about it."

Mrs. Percival stopped her machine and looked at her small girl with her sweet smile.

"It is a glad and happy land," she said, "with no sick or suffering people; no tears, no sin. It's a joyful place for little children."

"They don't sit in church praying and singing hymns all the time?"

"No, indeed they don't, Bee. Why should they? They can see their loving Saviour in all His glory. They can talk to Him, and sing to Him, of course, but it won't be in a church. I hear you singing about the house when you're happy, and that is how you will sing in heaven. I think even little children will be serving their Saviour."

"It's a *very* happy place, isn't it, Mums?"

"Yes, happier than we can imagine."

"I wonder every one doesn't *long* to go there."

Bee's tone was wistful. Then she jumped to her feet.

"May I take Jimmy some more story-books?"

"I think you might; but don't take any belonging to Babs or Bob, unless they allow you."

"They ought to like Jimmy to have them," said Bee in an injured tone.

Then she ran off to look through her books, and was very busy for the rest of the afternoon packing up a parcel to take to the sick boy.

The next afternoon Mrs. Percival and her three children walked out over the moor. They took their tea with them, and got into a pretty hollow by the side of a rushing stream, where they boiled a kettle, and picked whortleberries to make into jam. They enjoyed themselves immensely, and after tea Bee was allowed to go by herself to Agnes' cottage to see Jimmy. It was not very far away from them, and they could see the big chimney from where they were. Mrs. Percival had brought a book and some knitting; she told Bee that she need not hurry, for they could walk back in the cool of the evening.

Bee danced lightly over the heather. There was nothing she liked better than visiting people alone. When she got to the cottage she found that Agnes was out; she and her father had both gone off to the village to shop. Jimmy received her with a pleased smile.

"I've been longing to come, Jimmy. I thought I should never get here, and I've been finding out all about heaven, and everyone says the same about it."

"Country or town?" enquired Jimmy abruptly.

Bee hesitated.

"I fink it's both—houses to live in, and fields to play in. I'll tell you the people I've asked."

She gave an account of Mrs. Comfort, and of Mr. James Tolly.

Jimmy knew him and told her so.

"But I never have talked on heaven wi' 'im!"

He lay back in his small bed listening with glistening eyes to all that Bee could tell him.

" 'Tis nice to hear," he said, "when my back aches special I think o' all such things. But I be pretty sure as how I won't want to sit still up there. I shall be runnin' and jumpin' like mad. It will be grand to have proper legs and a straight back."

"You'll fly too, like the angels," said Bee dreamily; "that's what I shall like doing best. I often dream I am flying. Heaven is a kind of big Fairy Land, Jimmy, I fink."

The little boy nodded. "The hymn book tells an awful lot too about 'em—'There's a Friend for little children', do you know that 'un?"

"Yes." Bee's face brightened.

Jimmy began to count on his fingers.

"It says there be a 'Friend'—that's Jesus, 'a rest'—that be a nice bent covered wi' flowers I hope, a 'home'—that be a lovely house wi' a big garding, a 'crown'—that be for best occasions with pearls and rubies and sparklin' stones, a 'song'—that be a song which goes with harps and such like, and a 'robe'—white silk I should say. 'Harp' made o' gold, and 'palms' green and cool. Eight things I've counted, and all mine when I get there. Aggie put me in mind o' that hymn—her an' I du sing it proper on Sundays."

"We sing it too," said Bee; "I'll always think of you, Jimmy, when I sing it. Now look at these books I've brought you."

Her treasures were displayed on his bed, and they found a good deal to say to each other. Time slipped by, and then Bee felt she ought to say good-bye.

"You'll come again an' talk o' 'eaven to me," said Jimmy, holding out his wasted little hand; "it makes it more 'ome-like to go there, hearin' tell of it."

"I hope you won't go there just yet," said Bee looking at him gravely.

"Maybe when the winter comes I shall," said Jimmy quite calmly; "Doctor said as 'ow the winter up here were too rough for me, and the wind 'ee comes in like knives, can't kape it out no how! An' me lungs is all wrong, so he sez."

"I hope the winter won't come for a long time. Good-bye, Jimmy."

Bee left him, and trotted across the heather again.

Bob and Babs were still busy picking whortle-berries. Bee snuggled up against her mother, and laid her head on her shoulder.

"Jimmy simply loves heaven, Mums, but I feel I don't want to go just yet. There are so many things to do down here."

"Yes, my child, there are. But God wants you to be happy just where you are, and you can serve Him down here quite as well as up there. It is like Aunt Judy's ponies on the moor, they live out on it all day, and some of them are used to hard work, but in the evening they all trot home, they know where they're going, they know they have happiness and comfort before them. Your darling father went home when his day's work was over, and each one of us will be called in the same way, but if we belong to God down here, we shall know it is just going home to Him."

Bee nodded. She understood, and she began to talk of other things. Presently she joined the others in picking the whortleberries, and

when they went home they were able to give
Fanny a large basket of the fruit. She made it
into jam the very next day.

And then after a wonderful month of heat
and sunshine, the weather suddenly changed.
A Dartmoor gale blew for three days with slash-
ing rain. The springs and streams were swollen
and overflowed their banks. And though the wind
calmed down after a bit, the rain went on.

"Look, Mums," Bob cried one morning,
"look how high the water is getting! It's nearly
up to the bridge. The postman says it has been
washed away once. Wouldn't it be fun if it was
washed away now?"

"It would not be fun to us," said his mother;
"for we should not be able to get food from the
village."

"Oh yes, we would have a ferry-boat then!"

Bob dashed off to talk over matters with his
sisters. They all agreed that the prospect was
most exciting, and they watched the swollen
river rush along, hoping that every hour it
would rise higher and higher.

"And then Mums will really let me be a Christofferus I hope," said Bob. "I know how to swim
now, I've learnt. I could swim backwards and
forwards fifty times without getting tired."

His mother overheard him. She took him to
her bed-room window and told him to notice

quite a big tree that was being swirled along under the bridge.

"That shows you the force of the current, Bob. If you tried to swim in that water, you would be carried away for a certainty. You must not attempt to go into the water. You have had your lesson once, remember!"

Bob looked very disappointed. He and his sisters spent most of their time watching the rushing water from the windows. It was too wet to go out of doors, and the wind began to howl and bluster again. It seemed as if the rain and storm would never stop.

And the next morning Fanny came rushing up to her mistress's room.

"The bridge is clean gone, ma'am. It has bin carried right away in the night."

Of course the children were delighted. No postman or baker arrived, but when they went down to breakfast they saw a little group of men and boys the other side of the river, evidently discussing the situation. Though the rain was still heavy and the wind high, Fanny put on her waterproof and valiantly went down the lane to where the bridge had been. Fanny screamed to the men and they screamed to her, and after a lot of talking, she came back to the house with a relieved face.

"They've got a rope," she said, "and they're

fixing it to a post with a kind of pulley, and Smithson the carpenter is coming over this side, and going to fix it up this side, and when we or anyone in the lane want anything from the village, we can just haul our things over by the rope. They'll ring a bell to tell us when they're there. They did it last time there was no bridge."

"But why don't they get a boat?" demanded Bob.

"There was a accident last time, they say. A boy got drownded, the current is too strong, it's coming down from the moors like a rapid!"

This sounded delicious to the children. They implored their mother to let them go out when their meat and bread was brought to them, and she finally gave way. Wrapped in oilskin caps and coats she, and they, and Fanny, all went out, when they heard the bell ring.

A big basket from the general shop was sent over on the rope. In it were letters for Mrs. Percival, bread, and meat from the butcher. There were also several other parcels for other people and one big packet of groceries for Aunt Judy. Old Joe had come down on hearing about the bridge. He generally sent his boy with the daily milk that arrived from Miss Percival, but today he came himself.

"How are our ponies?" Bob asked him, "did

you bring back the ponies from the moor last night in all the rain?"

"Eh, bless me 'art no! 'Twas too rough for they. Us kep' un in all day yest'day. But this 'ere rope business be child's play. A good strong nag would weather through the water."

"Mums," cried Bob excitedly, "can't I go up and get Ran and ride over? He's so strong I'm sure he would do it."

"No, my boy, he wouldn't; look how the water is swirling along. No horse, least of all a small pony, could keep his footing. I don't think we need wait here any longer. Come into the house."

Much against their will the children were taken indoors.

And still the rain poured down, and the river rose higher and higher.

That evening when the children were in bed, Mrs. Percival sat in her room darning socks. Fanny was helping her with her mending basket. Gusts of wind shook the house.

"Hark!" cried Fanny suddenly.

There was a shrill cry outside, and a most awful crash.

They rushed to the window, but could see little.

"Help! Help!"

It was a woman's voice, and both Mrs. Percival and Fanny, throwing their waterproof coats round them, opened the front door and in spite of rain and wind ran through the garden and down to the river.

A reckless young motorist had dashed through the village at full speed, saw the broken bridge, tried to pull up, could not, and plunged right into the river. It was a young girl, and she was clinging to the seat of her car, half in and half out of the water.

"Help me!" she called out. "I can't move, fling me a rope!—anything for me to catch hold of!"

To Mrs. Percival's astonishment a voice by her side said:

"I'll swim in, and bring her over on my back. I won't be a minute. I'll be like Christofferus then."

It was Bob, in his overcoat over his pyjamas.

"I was awake, Mums. If only you'll let me go into the water, I'll fetch her over."

"Not to be thought of. *You*, Bob! It's ridiculous, my dear child!"

Bob sighed, then he brightened up.

"If she catches hold of the rope that brings the basket across, we can pull her over."

"Yes," said his mother, "I do believe you're right."

She called out directions to the girl, who put out her hands, and soon found and gripped

hold of the rope. Fanny and Mrs. Percival un-
fastened the pulley on their side of the river,
and began to haul the rope over. In a very few
minutes the girl was landed safely beside them,
but she sank down upon the ground in great
pain.

"It's my ankle—it's broken, I think!"

They managed to get her into the house.
Fanny lighted a fire in the sitting-room, and
Mrs. Percival brought down her own blankets
and put her upon the chintz-covered couch. They
got her into dry clothes, and gave her a hot
drink, but she was in great pain. Bob hovered
about wanting to help, and suddenly his mother
turned to him.

"You shall help, Bob. It is only half-past
eight, and I believe your Cousin Ted is dining
at the Hall tonight. Aunt Judy would telephone
there.

"Go steadily, and come straight back directly
your aunt has had the answer."

In a few minutes Bob was out of the house.
He felt very important, flashing his light here,
there, and everywhere, and rather enjoying the
darkness than otherwise. There was a high
wind but very little rain, and Bob reached his
aunt's house in safety. He gave a very big peal
to the bell, and loved it when Aunt Judy's
elderly servant, Ruth, came to the door with a

scared face, and screamed at the sight of him.

And then Aunt Judy came out.

"Who on earth is it? Not little Bob?"

"We've got a lady who tumbled into the river with her car," said Bob with dignity, "and she's very hurt; she's broken her leg or foot and she wants a doctor, and Mums thinks Cousin Ted is at the Hall, and will you please 'phone and tell him to come at once, and I'm to wait for his answer."

Aunt Judy did not waste a minute. She flew to her telephone. Ruth made Bob slip out of his damp coat, and took him into the comfortable kitchen, where after a few minutes Aunt Judy found him.

"Ted will come. I caught him," she said triumphantly; "tell me more about it, Bob."

So Bob told her all he knew, and then said he must go. His aunt did not keep him, but she said she would come round in the morning to see how things were.

"Your poor mother hasn't the room to house a stranger in. You don't know her name?"

Bob shook his head. Then he trotted off down the drive and along the lane. Suddenly his light went out; the battery was exhausted. He began to dislike the darkness.

"I'm not a bit like Offerus," he told himself. His momentary scare died away; but now came heavy footsteps up the lane.

Who was it? Bob stood close to the hedge. Men's voices came to his ear, and this is what he heard:

"Tell'ee, man, that the Squire be away nex' week, Toosday night be our chance—no moon now, and wind enough to hide the noise o' the tools. When I climbed the toolip tree outside her windy, I seed how the jools were flung about, and her in bed. And the flunkeys be in farthest wing away, so we needn't be feered o' they!"

They were coming close to him now; but he did not stir. He saw they looked like two slouching tramps. They passed him speaking in gruff undertones, but he had heard quite enough to know that they were up to no good, and he gave a little shiver as he thought that they might have discovered him, and then what would have happened!

He hurried home as fast as his legs could take him, and arrived very breathless, and pale. His mother was so concerned about her uninvited guest that she had no time to speak to him.

"Run off to bed, dear. You have helped me so much by going, but I cannot talk to you now."

Bob went to his little room very reluctantly. He was full of excitement over what he had heard, and longed to wake up Babs and Bee to tell them all about it, but there was one thing that their mother had positively forbidden, and that was for them to run in and out of each other's rooms after they had gone to bed. Happily he was both tired and sleepy, and when Cousin Ted arrived in his car twenty minutes later, Bob was already fast asleep.

CHAPTER NINE

MRS. PERCIVAL'S GUEST

THE girls were much excited the next morning to know that a stranger was in bed in their sitting-room. The children had their breakfast in the kitchen. Babs and Bee were very impressed with Bob's walk in the dark to fetch the doctor. While Fanny was getting their porridge ready, they crept out of doors down to the river. There was a group of villagers looking at the car, which was half in the water and half out, but none of them seemed inclined to do anything. The rain had at last stopped, but the river was very high, and was flooding a part of the lane. Mrs. Percival joined them at breakfast.

"Our visitor's name is Miss Ida Vaughan," she said in answer to their enquiries. "She does not live here, but was touring through Devon on a holiday. She has broken one of her ankle bones, and I don't want you to make a noise, for she is feverish and must be as quiet as possible. She's very unhappy about her car, but Cousin Ted said some of your uncle's workmen will come down this morning and see to it."

"Mums, I've something very very important to tell you," said Bob mysteriously. "I think I'd like to tell it to you in secret."

"I haven't much time for secrets today, Bob."

"But this is really a *horrible* secret," cried Bob; "you must listen."

Mrs. Percival looked at him hesitatingly, but after breakfast she took him off to her room and there was told of the two men in the dark, and of what they had said.

"You are sure you are telling me quite truly, Bob? You are not making it up, or exaggerating?"

"Mums, on my life and honour I'm not."

"Very well dear, I believe you. And we must let your Uncle Ralph know as soon as possible. He *is* going away next week, I know. Perhaps some of them may be over this morning?"

"But won't you go up and tell him at once? Mayn't I go? Do let me. I want to be useful, Mums."

Mrs. Percival hesitated again, then she said:

"Yes, I can trust you, but don't chatter about it. And tell your uncle before you tell anyone else."

Bob was delighted. When his sisters asked him where he was going, he said, with pursed up mouth:

"On a secret errand."

Bob was away a long time. And then Aunt Judy appeared to see how the invalid was. She brought a message, Bob was being kept to lunch at the Hall. She and Mrs. Percival were talking together in Mrs. Percival's bed-room. Bee noticed that the sitting-room door was ajar, and very softly she peeped in. Her curly head was hardly visible when a voice called out:

"Come in, little girl."

In Bee went, and stood at the end of the big couch looking at the invalid with a pleased smile.

"I'm just wanting distraction," she said in a happy laughing way. "Come and chatter to me. What do they call you?"

"Bee, but my real name is Beatrice. I fought you was too ill to talk."

"Not a bit of it! My tongue is whole and sound, thank goodness. What a beautiful young mother you have got! Quite like a fairy queen."

"Is she?"

This was a new idea to Bee. "Mums" was just "Mums". None of the children had ever thought her beautiful.

She regarded the invalid gravely.

"I wonder if you're very hurt, and if you'll always have to lie in bed on your back like Jimmy?"

"I don't know who Jimmy is."

"Jimmy's a very nice boy. He hasn't got a very long time to stay here, so he's getting ready for heaven as fast as he can."

"And how is he doing that?"

"Well, you see I read and tell him all I know about it. There's one fing he'd like to learn before he goes, so that he won't feel awkward 'mong the angels; but we don't know how he can do it."

"And what is that?"

"It's to play a harp. People don't seem to have many harps here. The village shop doesn't keep them—only penny whistles, and trumpets. Do you know anybody who plays a harp?"

But Miss Vaughan crumpled up her face, and gave a groan.

"A-a-ow! I'm a bad one to bear pain. I can't talk any more. Run away! But come again, and cheer me up!"

Bee crept out of the room and was caught in the act by her mother who was coming downstairs.

"Oh, Bee, that is naughty!"

"Oh, Mums, I only peeped in, and she told me to come in, and she's ever so nice, and—and I loves her!"

"Don't scold her," said Aunt Judy, with whom Bee was a prime favourite; "I'm sure if I were laid up on a couch, I'd welcome the sight of Bee's round face. Well, my dear Edie, I must go, but if you're going to keep her for a bit, I'll put up the chicks. Can't I? Won't you trust them to me?"

"I'd rather keep them here," said Mrs. Percival. "It's very good of you, but we shall manage."

Bee rejoined her sister in the kitchen.

"She's going to stay, Babs, isn't it fun! And I've been talking to her."

Presently their mother told them that they could go out for a walk.

"It has stopped raining. Put on your rubber boots, and walk up the lane as far as Joe Neale's cottage. He is going in to Newton tomorrow morning early, to bring out some groceries for Aunt Judy, and I want him to bring me some things too."

The little girls were delighted to get out of the house. The lane was very muddy, and there was a deep ditch along one side of it, in which the water was rushing down from the moor.

Joe's cottage was a dear little cottage, covered with roses outside, and the kitchen was a picture of cosiness and comfort. Mrs. Neale was a rosy smiling woman. The door was wide open and she and her husband were having their tea. There was a small bright fire in the shining black-leaded stove. Babs delivered her message and Joe pocketed the list, and said he would bring the things back.

" 'Tis a bad state of affairs, that there bridge bein' broke. But 'tis a massy the railway be over our side. The missis here will meet I wi' the pony cart, for I 'ave a goodly load to bring back."

"And won't our parcels come across by the rope?" asked Babs, "we love watching the basket being hauled over."

Joe laughed.

"Ay, the youngsters dearly love a mishap, don't they!"

"When shall we be able to ride again, Joe?" asked Bee. "I want to see Jimmy. Could we go on the moor tomorrow?"

"Surely no, missie. The moor be like a well-soaked sponge, and the boggy bits of un be dangerous sure enough!"

Bee looked disappointed. Then Mrs. Neale said:

"That be poor little Jimmy tu Wonnycot? I heerd tell yestern from James Tolly who come by there t'other day that Agnes an' her feyther went to Newton, an' the rain come on so fearful, that it drapped right away through roof, and pattered on Jimmy where he was by his lone self, an' he couldn't move, and they coom back an' foun' he wet through his shirt, an' shiverin', an' now he lies ill o' rheumaticky fever—and not like to pull through doctor says! But there, 'twill be a mercy I sez for the poor lil' lad to be taken. 'Tis only half a life he has lyin' on that bit bed."

"Oh I knew he would be ill, I knew he would be ill! I want to see him!"

Bee was very near tears, her voice rose in a wail.

"Come on home," said practical Babs, "and we'll tell Mums about him."

They set off home. Bee was inconsolable.

"Poor, poor Jimmy! Lying in bed, and the rain drip, drip, dripping on him! And getting soaked and wet and no ombrella, nor nuffing to keep his face dry. And getting colder, and wetter, and colder, and nobody there to warm him!"

When her mother promised to do something in the matter, Bee cheered up. They had their tea in the kitchen, and Bob arrived before it was over. He was very pleased with himself, and was proud now to disclose his secret.

"Uncle Ralph is actually going to give me a rabbit, a real live rabbit!"

"Why?" demanded Babs.

Bob held his head very erect.

"Because I've saved his house from a burglary, and next Tuesday there's going to be grand doings up at the Hall. The police will be hiding, and the thieves will come, and there may be a regular scrimmage and fight! Pistols, and all that, and Harry means to be in it, and I only wish I could be! But as I'm being given a rabbit, I can't ask for more than that!"

"Whatever are you talking about?" asked Babs.

Then Bob told them the whole story.

"And when I got up to the Hall, Uncle Ralph told me he couldn't be bothered with me, so I stepped up close to him, and said in his ear in a *very* loud whisper:

" 'It's thieves and murder; and Aunt Eva will be murdered while you're away! And I'm not joking, on my soul and honour I aren't!'

"So then he listened to me. And first he pretended not to believe me, and then he did, for he said there were two men living in a ruined cottage close to the moor, and they were doubtful characters! That's what he called them. And of course it must be them, and if they're caught, I'm to have the rabbit!"

"But perhaps they won't be caught!" said Babs.

Bob refused to think of that possibility. He was very full of his burglars, and could talk of nothing else for the rest of the day.

Just after tea, Mrs. Percival told Bee she might come in and see the invalid.

"She's been asking for you, but you must be very quiet, and only stay quite a short time."

Bee crept in as quiet as a little mouse. Miss Vaughan was sitting up propped against cushions.

"Where's your home?" Bee asked her.

"In London."

"That's where we've comed from. Do you live in a very big house?"

"In one big room," said Miss Vaughan, laughing. "I'm very poor, Bee, and I earn my living by painting. At least I have tried to do it, but I can't get enough money to save me from starvation, and so I'm going to give it up —in fact I've given notice to my landlady already. A rich friend of mine lent me her car to have a holiday in it, and this is how I have repaid her! Smashed her car to pieces, and smashed my ankle." She laughed, as she met Bee's pitying blue eyes.

"Mums says we're poor, but not poor enough to be unhappy, and you aren't either, are you?"

"No, I never could be unhappy," said Miss Vaughan; "it isn't in me. I think your mother's quite rich—to have a darling house like this, and three small children to keep her lively, and a faithful maid-servant."

Bee climbed down from her seat, and crept up close to Miss Vaughan.

"I like you very much," she said taking hold of one of Miss Vaughan's hands and laying it against her cheek. "I hope you will stay here a long time."

"What! Keep you out of this pretty sitting-room as I am doing! I'm sure the others wish me gone. As for your mother, if you like *me*, I adore her! I think she's a perfect angel!"

The door opened and the "angel" appeared. Bee's allotted time was over and she had come to tell her so.

"No," Mrs. Percival said firmly, when Miss Vaughan begged that she should stay longer. "As long as you are feverish you must be kept quiet. My little people chatter too much. Bee shall come and see you again tomorrow."

So Bee said good-night, and in bed that evening tossed about before she went to sleep, thinking of Jimmy and of Miss Vaughan by turns.

The next morning Agnes appeared, and asked especially to see "Miss Bee". "Jimmy asked me to come," she said.

"Oh, how is he?" asked Bee breathlessly, "is he going to heaven?"

Agnes looked sober.

"I 'ope as 'ow he bain't! But I'm orful miserable!" Here she began to cry.

Bee immediately joined her.

"He is going then, and I shan't see him any more."

"He's gone!" sobbed Agnes, "he went yesterday, and I dunno what I'll do without him."

"Gone to heaven!" gasped Bee; "but you said you hoped he wasn't going."

"He be gone to the doctor's. Doctor Ted, him what belongs to you, he come up, an' he sez as how he must be praper nursed, an' that I couldn't do un praper! An' he come an' talked to Feyther, and they wrapped Jimmy up in blankets and took 'un in Doctor's car to his house, and Mrs. Comfort be going to look arter 'im."

Bee stopped crying and clapped her hands.

"Oh how lovely, Agnes! Then he'll get well. Jimmy staying with Cousin Ted, and having Mrs. Comfy to nurse him! Aren't you glad, won't you be if he gets better?"

Agnes would not be comforted.

"I've done for Jimmy ever since mother died, an' he an' I get on splendid. 'Tis lonesome wi'out 'im, an' Feyther away all day."

Very soon Dr. Ted arrived. He visited Miss Vaughan first, and found her much better.

"You and I," said Mrs. Percival to him, "are both entertaining sick people. How good of you to take the little boy from Wonnycot! Are you going to send him to hospital?"

"No, I'll keep him with me, and see what can be done for him. Old Comfy loves children, and just revels in nursing."

"Is he very bad?"

"Just escaped rheumatic fever, but I have an idea that when he is fairly well, we can give him some special treatment. I've seen marvellous cures—of course he'll have to go to hospital for that, but I want to feed him up first and get some flesh on his bones."

"His little sister is here, and very unhappy and anxious about him."

"She need not be."

Cousin Ted came out into the garden. Bee and Agnes were standing by the gate expectantly waiting for him.

"How's Jimmy?" he said cheerily; "why, he's first rate. He'll be sitting up again in a few days. Would you like to come and see him? Jump into my car and I'll drive you back with me."

Agnes turned rosy with delight. She climbed into the car with shining eyes, and drove off amidst cheers from Babs and Bob and Bee.

Bee turned to her mother.

"Oh, Mums, you said I could keep a chicken farm when I growed up, but I fink I shall be a lady doctor and make sick people well. Fancy! only fancy! if Cousin Ted was to make Jimmy walk! Wouldn't it be wunnerful!"

CHAPTER TEN

THE PICNIC

THERE was much excitement in the neighbourhood the following Tuesday, when the police did manage to capture the two housebreakers. Uncle Ralph was very grateful to his nephew, and true to his promise sent him a pair of beautiful rabbits with a large and comfortable hutch.

Bob was delighted. He spent all his time with his pets, and Babs and Bee were only too willing to help him in cleaning out their house, and providing them with food and drink. The river had subsided; a new bridge was made, and life flowed on as evenly as before.

But Miss Vaughan was still at the Ferry House. She had been given Bob's small room, and Bob had been moved into the box-room. The children grew very fond of her; she was always full of fun, and though she could not walk yet, she never seemed impatient or discontented.

And then one day their mother sprang a surprise upon them. She and Aunt Judy and

Miss Vaughan had been having consultations together. And the surprise was this. Miss Vaughan was going to stay with them altogether and be the little girls' governess.

Babs looked rather serious when she heard of this.

"But she isn't a governess, Mums, she paints pictures."

"Pictures which she can't sell, poor girl!" said Mrs. Percival; "but she has had a college education and knows a great deal more than I do, Babs. It will give me more time for gardening and for sewing. The days are not half long enough for all I want to do."

"It will be lovely," said Bee ecstatically, "now we shall never say good-bye to her."

She ran off at once to Miss Vaughan and flung her arms round her neck.

"You'll be in our family now and never leave us! And if we learns our lessons with you, you'll play with us and tell us stories after! Isn't it puffickly lovely!"

"I won't be a dragon of a governess, Bee sweetest, I promise I won't. We'll do lessons furiously till lesson time is over and then we'll play for all that we are worth."

"And now what shall we call you?" Bee asked.

"I have a very short name that I used to be called by my brothers, when I was young. I should like to hear that name again, It's 'Dew'."

"Why did they call you that?"

"Oh I think it was because I was a tearful child, they used to chaff me about my dewdrops."

Miss Vaughan looked rather sad.

"I have nobody to call me 'Dew' now."

"We'll call you 'Dew' as often as we can," said Bee, putting her arms again round Miss Vaughan's neck, and looking into her face very earnestly.

The children accepted her as governess at once. But lessons did not begin just yet. One day just before the holidays were over, Harry invited them out for a moor picnic.

"It's a riding picnic," he told Bob, "everybody is coming on horses, and we're going ten miles out. Dad and Mother and some of their friends are coming too. We shall have lunch at the top of one of the Tors."

"And shall we carry our picnic on our ponies?"

Harry gave a scornful laugh.

"The servants will take that in one of our cars. We don't do those kind of things when we have servants to do it for us."

"I carried a tin of oil for an old woman yesterday," said Bob reflectively. "I was on my pony, and she could hardly get along. It banged against me dreadfully and spilt a little!"

"What did you do it for, you duffer!"

"Oh well, I have to do it, you know. I told you about Offerus, didn't I? I'm going to be like him. I don't mind being a kind of servant to people, because if I serve them, I serve the strongest King in the world. Mums says we're all servants, or we ought to be if we're not."

"I never mean to be, *never*," said Harry, "they shall serve me always. I wasn't born a servant, and I'll never make myself into one."

Harry ran off with a laugh.

"If you're so fond of carrying things," he called out from a distance, "you can carry my fishing tackle and basket. I'm going to catch trout and cook them for tea out on the moor."

Bob could make no reply, for Harry was out of sight, and perhaps it was just as well that he was.

The day of the picnic dawned beautifully bright. The children's ponies and their mother's were brought down to the house by Joe, who told them that their Aunt Judy was going to join them on the moor in time for tea. They set off, a very happy little party. Mrs. Percival knew the way, and when they reached the moor, they saw in the distance some other riders coming from the direction of the Hall. And then suddenly Mrs. Percival stopped.

"I've actually come away without giving Fanny the money I promised her. She's going into Newton. I'm afraid I shall have to go back and join you later."

"I'll go back, Mums," said Bob promptly, "I love a gallop, and so does Ran. You give me the money, and I'll get back home in no time."

"Will you, dear boy? That's very kind of you. I think you will be able to overtake us. You see the Tor we're making for?"

"Yes, I know it quite well."

So Mrs. Percival got out her purse and put fifteen shillings into Bob's hand.

"Tell Fanny I'm very sorry for my forget-fulness."

Bob went off. He was always willing to do his mother's messages, so she and the little girls went on. The heather was already turning purple, and the bracken was edged with gold. They were almost sorry when their ride over the heather was over, but the little girls were de-lighted to meet some other children who had driven over in a car, and there were so many people at the rendezvous and so much laughing and talking, that for the time Bob was quite forgotten. His mother remembered him, how-ever, when lunch was spread out on the ground, and he was still absent. She grew uneasy, and wondered if he had lost his way. When she expressed her fears to her brother-in-law, he laughed.

"Bob can take care of himself anywhere. I wish my Harry had his good common sense. He'll be here presently. We'll see that some lunch is kept for him."

Lunch was over, and it was a big meal, and had taken a full hour in its process, but there was no Bob.

Mrs. Percival did not enjoy herself any more. She was anxious about her boy. Some of the men and boys went fishing, the little girls played about on the moor with the other children. A few of the older ladies and herself settled themselves with books and needlework under the shadow of the great blocks of granite that were piled in heaps upon the crest of the Tor. But presently she got up, and said that she would ride a part of the way back to see whether Bob was coming.

When she had gone about three or four miles, she met Aunt Judy coming along in her pony chaise.

"Have you seen or heard anything of Bob?" Mrs. Percival asked her eagerly.

"Joe met him a couple of hours ago; he had been home with some message, had he not? And he was cantering up the lane back to the moor at a great pace."

"He has never appeared," said Mrs. Percival; "where can he be?"

She turned her mare's head. It was of no use going home. Bob must be somewhere out on the moor.

"Don't worry," advised Miss Percival; "the boy is a born rider. Perhaps he may have missed his way. He'll be with the picnic party by now, I expect."

But when they reached the others, he was still absent.

And then when tea was in full swing, Mrs. Percival looked up, and in the distance saw a little figure on his pony. It was Bob at last. When he came up, he looked tired and forlorn.

Harry ran to meet him at once.

"You're a nice one playing truant from our picnic, as if you didn't care to come."

"Shut up!" said Bob crossly, "I couldn't help it."

But he wouldn't tell anyone what he had been doing, only said that he had gone home on a message, and got delayed coming back. His mother was so thankful to see him safe and sound that she asked him no questions, and plied him with tea and cakes. Only a few had noticed his absence, and his uncle concluded that he had missed his way over the moor.

It was not until they were riding home alone, when the picnic was over, that Bob gave his mother a full account of himself.

"I got home all right, and Fanny was awfully glad to see me and get her money. Then I came straight back, but when I was half way across the moor, I came upon that old tinker Bee talks about—James Tolly. He was kneeling in the road by the side of his horse. His cart was there with all its pots and pans, but wasn't it awful, Mums! His horse had stumbled and died! He was very very old, and Mr. Tolly said he'd been off his feed, but he was crying like anything, said he'd never have driven him till he dropped, if he'd known he was really bad. And he didn't seem to know what to do. And no one was near. He said if he walked off and left his cart, his pots and pans would be stolen, and he wanted to get to the next village. And we talked about it, and then we thought Ran would pull the cart to the village if we walked, so we did that, and left the poor old horse where he was. Mr. Tolly said he would go back to him, as soon as his pots and pans were safe. Ran was very tiresome at first, and then he settled down, but it took us a long while to get to the village, and I had to wait till he had found someone to put up his cart, and then the man there said Ran would be the better for a feed and a drink before I started off again, so I had some bread and cheese, Mums, and a bottle of ginger beer, for I knew I wouldn't be here in time for dinner, and then coming back, I took a wrong turn and went for miles out of my way. I thought I should never find you. I feel quite tired out!"

"Why did you stop for that old man?" questioned Babs; "I would have come straight here, and sent one of Uncle Ralph's men-servants to help him. There were two of them doing nothing but laying the lunch."

"But I was the one to help him," said Bob; "because I found him. Wasn't I, Mums? Offerus would have taken him on his back, I know he would, and though I couldn't do that, I could lend him my pony."

"You did quite right, Bob dear," said his mother; "I would have done the same myself, had I been in your place."

"I nearly didn't," confessed Bob, looking at his mother with earnest eyes; "I wanted to get to the picnic awfully, but I knew quite well I mustn't!"

"Poor Mr. Tolly," said tender-hearted Bee; "how drefful to lose his horse! Will he give him a funeral?"

"The policeman said a farmer would go out and bring him in a cart and bury him," said Bob; "but Mr. Tolly was feeling bad. I wonder if Aunt Judy has an old horse she could spare him. He said he could never afford to buy another."

The children were greatly interested in Bob's adventure. They even consulted together as to whether they could make a collection in the village for James Tolly. Bee produced three-pence halfpenny, and Babs fivepence, and Bob emptied his money box which held in it one shilling and twopence. Fanny said she would subscribe sixpence. But when they went to their mother to ask her if they could go through the village and collect subscriptions, she said she would talk to the rector about it.

Mrs. Percival did talk to the rector, and to Miss Percival; and Harry's father took the matter up, and before lessons began, James Tolly was starting his rounds again with another horse.

He came one day himself to thank Mrs. Percival for her kindness in helping him.

"And as to the lil' master," he said when talking to her, "he be a reg'lar wonder for his age! Talked to me of a Popish chap wi' a saint to his name. I never heerd tull o' 'ee! But he seemed to think as he were a follerin' in his footsteps sure enough! An' if it be his work to lift the burdens o' others, 'tis pretty sartain he lifted wan off I!"

Mrs. Percival was pleased to hear this about her son, but she did not say much to Bob; she was so afraid of making him self-conscious and conceited. She took it for granted now that he should be always ready when the opportunity came of helping those in trouble or distress.

"If you are a King's servant, Bob," she said, "you will be His messenger, and He has put His servants in this world to minister to those in trouble."

Bob nodded; he never said much, but he was certainly acting out his creed. And he was a happier boy in consequence.

CHAPTER ELEVEN

HARRY'S NEWS

THE holidays were over. Lessons went briskly. Bee adored her governess and Babs liked her. Dew had no trouble with either of them. They worked hard from nine till one. In the afternoon they went for long walks, sometimes for rides with their mother. On these occasions Dew stayed at home; she could not ride and did not want to learn, and she was always glad of a quiet time to herself.

On one or two afternoons Bee had ridden over to her Cousin Ted's to see Jimmy, who still lay in bed in a pretty room overlooking the moor. His face had filled out, and he was stronger and better in every way. Good food and careful nursing had made him look quite a different boy. He was very soon going to a hospital in Plymouth, where Cousin Ted hoped great things would be done for him.

Bee and Jimmy still had long talks about the unseen Country which he had so nearly entered.

" 'Tis funny," Jimmy said to her one afternoon, "how I didn't seem to care nothin' for this 'ere earth; I were so awful close to heaven that I could talk and think o' nothin' else. And now I be thinkin' o' me mate, an' me clothes, an' of gettin' out in Doctor's car. Oh, it be just lovely when us sail along cross the moor wi' the blue sky and birds, an' the breeze blowin' tu our faces! An' Doctor sez if I don't never have the use o' mc legs, he thinks me back'll stiffen up, and maybe I'll sit up, and get about in a wheeled chair. Why, that be a wonderful thing for me, b'ain't un?''

"Yes," said Bee with a little sigh, "I'm very, very glad you're going to live here, Jimmy, and Agnes will be very glad, but it was very exciting —you must say it was—when you were so close to the golden gates, that any day you might be called in!''

Jimmy lay with a dreamy look in his dark eyes.

"Aye, I used to dream an' dream of what it would be like, an' when they brought me here, I seemed in a fair maze. There was a bit of time when I knewed nothing. I never felt or saw 'em bring me, an' when I woke up and found meself in this pretty room, and heard a wonderful bird sing—'twas Mrs. Comfort's canary—I thought I'd woke up in heaven—an' I said to myself, ' 'Tis all real nateral like it 'twas in the world I died in.' But I were quite sure I'd got through the gates.''

"I s'pose you were disappointed?"

"Just a bit, but I ain't now. I want to grow up and work for Dad and Agnes. Doctor says I could learn shoemakin'—or basket-makin' or mendin' china, and pots and pans like old Tolly. If these 'ere doctors in 'ospital will only make me sit up, 'stead o' lyin' on me back, why there be nothin' that I b'aint good for!"

And then came the day when Jimmy was taken to the hospital, and for a time Bee and Agnes heard very little about him, except that he was going on well, and that his was a hopeful case.

The days grew colder, and shorter and darker.

As winter drew on, Dew was invaluable with her ideas of arts and crafts. She taught the little girls to make raffia baskets, to paint calendars for Christmas and the New Year, and to make pretty bags and pincushions out of scraps of silk and leather.

One afternoon, Dew went into Newton Abbot to do some shopping with Aunt Judy in her car. Mrs. Percival came downstairs about half-past-three, and found Babs standing disconsolate by the sitting-room window. Her mother took her accustomed chair by the fire, then held out her hand to Babs.

"Come and sit down on this stool by me. What a cheerful room this is! I always think that bright fires make people cheerful. Where is Bee?"

"She's gone to see Joe's wife's little niece who's burnt her leg and is in bed. She took her one of our old story books."

"And Bob has not come in yet?"

"Yes, he has."

A dark frown gathered on Bab's face.

"He's taken the wheelbarrow and gone to get some sticks from the wood for old John Durdle. He met him hobbling home today, and said he couldn't stoop from rheumatics. I wish— I wish—"

"Well what do you wish?"

"I wish Bob had never heard of that old Offerus. He's always doing things for someone and won't play with me as he used to. I'm miserable, Mums. I'm always alone now—I have to do everything by myself. Bee is as bad as Bob, she's always making new friends and going to see them, and taking them things! And Bob won't do what I tell him, as he used to do. He seems quite a different kind of boy."

"And are Bob and Bee miserable?"

"No, of course they're not, they're enjoying themselves, but I'm not."

"My dear little Babs, you can make yourself quite happy by following their example. None of us is ever happy if we're only thinking about ourselves. I have often wondered that it never

133

enters your head to do things for others. You do things for me, I know, but you don't like giving Fanny any help, and if you met any village girl or boy in distress out of doors, you would not try to help them, would you?"

"I haven't a chance," muttered Babs; "Bob and Bee rush at them first."

"But you can run faster than they, and you're quicker than Bee in doing things. It's your heart, childie, that is wrong. A willing heart makes willing hands and feet. As you know, in London your daddy and I spent our lives in looking after poor people. I like to think my children have some of their father's spirit in them which makes them quick to see the needs of others. If you feel lonely why don't you find someone to go and see—or someone to help?"

"I can't, Mums, and I don't make friends in a minute like Bee. I can't go round, and knock at people's doors, and ask them if they want anything. Things happen to Bob and Bee, they never happen to me."

"I happen to know that there is an old blind woman in the village called Mrs. Martha Drake. She loves to be read to. Would you like to go to her, Babs darling?"

Babs did not answer. Her brow was puckered, she gazed into the fire, and would not look up at her mother.

Then after a minute or two she said slowly:

"Would you be pleased if I went, Mums?"

"I don't want you to do that kind of thing to please me. But, my child, if you want to please your Saviour, He says He wants His children to visit the poor and sick, and help those who are in need of help."

"I'll try, Mums. Shall I go tomorrow?"

So the next day, hugging a poetry book under her arm, Babs went in to read to Mrs. Drake.

She found her sitting in a big armchair by her fire. When she explained who she was, the old woman smiled.

Babs had a very pretty clear little voice, and she read a long poem of a woman and a child who were lost in a snowstorm and finally rescued by a big dog. Mrs. Drake nodded and smiled, and threw up her hands in horror as the poem proceeded. When it was finished, she said how much she had enjoyed it.

And then she told Babs of a story of her youth when she had had to find her way home through a blizzard.

Babs was so interested that her time slipped away before she was ready for it. And Mrs. Drake was so delighted with her reading that she begged her to come again soon.

" 'Tis a weary aye to sit and sit wi'out a soul tu spake tu. Me husband, he be workin' on farm still, an' he doan't come home till nightfall."

Babs ran home with a light heart; she began to find that doing things for someone else was more satisfactory than doing it for oneself. And Mrs. Percival, who had been afraid that her eldest daughter was growing selfish, was even more pleased than Babs herself.

A short time after this, Bob came home one day, and gave his sisters some news.

"Harry is going to school after Easter, and Uncle Ralph and Aunt Eva are going to live in London."

"What will you do then?" said Babs. "You'll have to do lessons with us."

"Shall I?"

Bob's tone was scornful, then he turned to his mother:

"What shall I do, Mums? Did you know Harry was going to school?"

"Yes, I did," said Mrs. Percival quietly, "I have known it for some time. Your uncle has told me all about it. And he wants me to send you to the same school."

"And where is it, Mums?"

"In Hampshire. Nothing is settled, Bob. I always believe in telling you children simple facts. I can't afford to pay for your schooling, but your uncle wants to do it. And I think I shall let him do it, for it is a good school, and will give you a good chance of getting on."

Babs and Bee did not like this separation from their brother; and they did not like his being so pleased about it.

"You won't have a pony to ride there," they told him; "and you won't be able to keep rabbits."

"I shall play hockey and football, and cricket instead," Bob retorted.

"And you won't be able to play at being Offerus there," said Babs a little spitefully.

Bob looked at her.

"You don't know anything about boys' schools, so you needn't pretend you do," he said.

"Hush, don't quarrel," said their mother.

"But, Mums, will the Hall be shut up? It will be horrid for us," said Babs; "we love going there, 'specially in the summer. But I suppose Harry will be home again by that time."

Mrs. Percival did not answer. The next day Harry came to tea. It was Bob's proposal, and Harry always enjoyed his time at the Ferry House. The smallness and snugness of it in contrast to his big home was an amusing change.

He arrived however with big eyes and a tragic face.

"Dad has been talking to me," he said, when he and his cousins were alone together. Fanny was out, and Mrs. Percival and Dew were in the kitchen getting the tea ready, and making some hot tea cakes for the occasion.

"And Dad and Mother are going abroad, and our house is going to be let to people for seven years! It's a beastly shame!"

Bob and the girls looked at him in consternation.

"Oh, Harry!" cried Babs; "how awful! You'll never come back here again for seven years!"

"Perhaps I may come to Aunt Judy's, but I shan't want to come to her if some horrible people are in our house."

"Why is it going to be given to other people?" asked Bee.

"Mother doesn't like the country, and some old uncle has died and left her his house in London, and she wants to live there half the year, and the other half abroad. And Dad says he's lost money, and can't keep the house here empty."

"And we shan't see you any more!" said Babs.

Bee linked her arm in Harry's, and cuddled against him affectionately. She did not dare to kiss him, for Harry hated kisses, but she showed how sorry she was for him.

"You poor boy!" she said. "You'll have to

leave your pony and the dogs and your nest in the tree, and your pet owls, and everyfing you love. You'll be as poor as us I 'spect."

"I shan't be poor at all!"

Harry twisted himself away from her as he spoke.

"As if I ever *could* be as poor as you are!"

"Being poor isn't at all bad," said Bob; "we're just as happy as you every bit. You're always so scornful of us, but we're as good as you."

Harry stared at him.

"Yes," said Babs, rubbing it in; "Fanny says if our father had been born before yours instead of after, we'd have been up at the Hall, and you'd have been down here. Then we would have said: 'Poor Harry, he's in such a poky house and has such shabby clothes that we're quite ashamed he's our cousin!' "

Harry turned very red, for this was one of his speeches soon after his cousins came to live at the Ferry House.

"Anyhow," he said; "I believe I'd rather be poor like you and stay on here, than leave the house for seven years. I shall be soon leaving school by that time—and none of my holidays will be at the Hall."

"Come and stay with Aunt Judy, and then we'll see you," said Bob. But Harry would not be comforted. After tea Dew insisted upon dressing them all up and acting charades, and Harry enjoyed this so much that he forgot his troubles. But when he was going home he poured out his story again into Mrs. Percival's ears. She felt very sorry for Harry.

"It is only for a time that it will be away from you. And Harry, dear, as you get older you will find that it isn't having possessions that makes us happy, but having a cheerful happy heart. You can have that anywhere."

"I thought," faltered Harry, "that I might bring one of the fellows at school home in the holidays, and now I shall have no home to bring them to!"

"Perhaps some of them may ask you to go with them instead," said Mrs. Percival.

But this was not at all the same thing to Harry.

He went off unconsoled. Dew said after he had gone:

"He'll have the chance of his life now, of proving himself to be a man. He is a spoilt bragging child at present."

"Yes," said Mrs. Percival gravely; "I am glad that riches have not spoiled my children. One wants to have other values than money and property."

Babs heard this conversation and asked the meaning of it.

"It's a question of what is really worth while in life, Babs," said her mother; "of what is most valuable and best in every way for people, and a lot of money and big houses and property are not the best things in life."

"What are, Mums?"

"A humble trust in God and a happy contented mind," said her mother, and Babs said no more.

CHAPTER TWELVE

DISASTER ON THE MOOR

"MUMS, can I ride out with Harry this afternoon?"

It was Saturday when Bob made this request.

"Where are you going?" his mother asked.

"Out on the moor. Harry is alone at home, and he's tired of playing about in the garden, and we haven't had a ride for days, it has been so wet."

"I have no objection, but don't get tripped up by rabbit holes, and don't be out after dark."

Babs and Bee were going to the woods with Dew to get some pine cones. They loved bringing them in and toasting them before the fire. They made such a pleasant aromatic scent in the room.

Mrs. Percival was going to tea with Aunt Judy, and when she got there they had a good talk over the affairs at the Hall.

"I'm sorry for Harry," said Mrs. Percival, "because he really adores his home here, but he is not taking it at all well. He sulks, and is rude to his mother about it. It is a very unhappy state of things. I'm quite ready to have him here in the holidays while his parents are abroad, but I am afraid he will fret a good deal at being shut out of the Hall."

"I think he may grow up a nicer boy from not having everything all his own way," said Mrs. Percival.

"Yes, he may. I think your Bob is worth two of him. I'm always glad when they're together."

Mrs. Percival did not return home till late, and she was rather annoyed to find that Bob had not appeared.

"He may have gone to tea with Harry," suggested Babs.

And as this was probable, Mrs. Percival did not feel anxious.

But at eight o'clock down came the Squire himself. Neither boys nor ponies had turned up.

"Ten to one," he said with a smile to Mrs. Percival, "your boy has been leading mine into some knight errantry. They've run against some vagabond tramp wanting a lift home. But it's not much fun to those expecting them. I am afraid there's a mist coming on. I think I shall ride out with Joe and take our lanterns."

He did so, and Mrs. Percival sat and waited. The little girls' bedtime came. Dew went upstairs with them, and then came down and sat with Mrs. Percival.

"I think they will be all right. They have gone further than they intended, and then when dusk came on missed their way."

"They may have met with an accident," said Mrs. Percival.

They grew more and more anxious as time went on. Nine o'clock, ten o'clock, and still no news. Then she sent both Dew and Fanny to bed, but waited on by herself, praying that both boys might be kept safe from harm or hurt.

Meanwhile, Bob and Harry had ridden happily enough across the moor. Harry had heard that a fox and cubs had been seen amongst the rocks near the crest of a certain Tor, and both boys were anxious to see if they could find any traces of them. It was a long ride, and they were longer poking about among the great granite slabs than they meant to be. They did not meet with any success, and turned their ponies' heads homewards. As Dew surmised dusk had overtaken them, and they missed the right track. Then up came a mist creeping round them, and raising an invisible wall between them and distant land marks.

"I say, we shall be lost!" exclaimed Harry, "we've got into the boggy parts, and we never touched them coming."

"I can't think why our ponies don't know

their way home," said Bob, "they ought to by this time."

"Let's give them their heads and see what they'll do."

But the plan did not seem to answer. Both ponies ambled on, then got slower and slower in their pace, and finally came to a standstill.

Harry lost patience, dug his heels into his pony's sides, and set off at a smart trot in the direction which he thought was right. Bob followed him, but the road was rough and uneven.

Suddenly there was a sharp cry from Harry, his pony went down and he was shot over his head. To Bob's horror he seemed to disappear from sight. When he dismounted and got the pony to his feet again, nowhere could he see his cousin.

"Harry! Harry! Where are you!" he shouted.

He fancied he heard a groan; grasping the reins of both ponies he cautiously walked forwards, then dislodged a stone, and heard a sudden splash. He started back just in time to save himself, for he was on the edge of an old gravel pit. For a moment he stood still, wondering what he had better do. If he quitted hold of the ponies, he might lose them. If he kept hold of them there was no hope of rescuing Harry. If he had been able to find a tree near, he could have tethered the ponies to it, but as it was, there was not even a bush or a twig to be found.

Then with delight, he remembered he possessed a small electric torch. Taking it out of his pocket, he was able to see his bearings. He saw that on one side he could scramble down to the bottom of the gravel pit, so he let the ponies go and began the descent. He tumbled and slid, and scrambled down, grazing his hands, and knees, but he got to the bottom at last. And then flashing his light on, he saw that there was a deep pool, and half in and half out was the unconscious form of poor Harry. When he reached him, it was a hard task to pull him out. He had fallen on his face, and it was a wonder that he was not already drowned, but he was groaning, though half unconscious. Bob had to stand waist deep in the water before he could get him out, and when he had laid him on dry ground, from the way one leg was bent beneath him he knew that it must be broken. Never in his life had Bob felt more helpless. He tried to drag Harry up the slope which he had come down, but the movement and the pain brought consciousness to the sufferer, and he almost screamed in his agony.

"Let me alone. I'm dying!"

Bob laid him down gently, took off his own

coat, and put it over Harry, for it was getting very cold.

"Harry, I must go for help!"

"Don't leave me. I'm dying, I shall die, oh, don't leave me!"

Harry gasped these words out, and clutched at Bob's hand.

Bob sat down by him, shivering himself with his wetting, and with the loss of his coat, wondering again what he had better do. Then he rose to his feet.

"I won't leave you, Harry—can you hear me? I'll only climb up to the top and fix my light somewhere to bring people to us. They're sure to come and look for us. I'll give a good 'Halloo', too, when I get up there, and then I'll come back to you. I won't leave you, I promise I won't! If the ponies haven't gone, I'll try and get them down here, or one of them at least, and perhaps I could lift you on his back. I'll see. I'll come back."

Harry groaned.

"Don't leave me."

But Bob with his good common sense scrambled up to the top of the pit, found a bit of fencing to which he fixed his torch, and then he sent up a loud cry for help. Again and again his shouts rang out across the silent misty moor; when he was hoarse with shouting he began

147

calling to Ran his pony, but there was no sign or sound of any ponies near.

He found his way back to Harry. He lay groaning, but seemed partly unconscious: he did not speak or make any response when Bob spoke to him. And Bob could do nothing but crouch by his side till help came, or the mist would roll away. Under his breath he murmured again and again:

"O God, help us! Send help to us!"

He never prayed harder or more earnestly in his life.

And then suddenly he heard the toot of a motor horn, and knew that there must be some good moor road near them, and a road meant possible rescue and help. He scrambled up to the top of the pit again. In the distance he saw two headlights, but were they going away or coming near? He rushed towards them, shouting loudly as he went. The lights slowed down. Bob knew then that help was near, but his limbs were shaking with excitement when a man's voice called out:

"Hullo! Who's there?"

And then the car stopped, and Bob had reached it.

It was no stranger. Just the man above all others who would be the most help. Dr. Ted.

"Is it Bob Percival? How come you here, my

boy? I saw a light in the distance, and guessed that somebody was in trouble. And then I fancied I heard somebody shouting, so I came along as fast as I could."

"Oh, come to Harry quick! He says he's dying, and his legs are all doubled up, and he doesn't speak now, only groans! He tumbled off his horse down a deep pit."

"The old gravel pit! Are we close to it? You lead the way."

In a very few minutes, the young doctor was by the side of the injured boy. His deft skilful fingers soon got the injured leg straightened out, and in rough temporary splints. Harry seemed quite unconscious. Dr. Ted brought him carefully up in his arms and laid him full length on the seat in his car. Then Bob was told to get in, and the car drove slowly over the moor in the direction of the Hall. They met the squire and some of his men on the outskirts of the moor.

It was nearly eleven o'clock before Dr. Ted took Bob to the Ferry House. He had stayed to set poor Harry's broken leg, and plaster up his cut head. He had comforted his father's heart by telling him that there was no danger, but that Harry might have a high temperature, and must be kept very quiet till he saw him again. The ponies were still straying over the moor, but Joe said they would find their way home when the mist had cleared.

Mrs. Percival had heard the car and was at her gate to meet her boy. She asked Dr. Ted to come in, but he would not, as he wanted to get home.

"Oh, Bob, Bob, my dearest boy, I have been so frightened and anxious. Are you all right yourself? What has happened?"

Bob told his story, sitting over the fire, after his mother had made him take off his wet clothes.

"Oh, Mums, it was awful at the bottom of that pit! It made me feel like Joseph! And I longed to be strong like Offerus. If only I had been stronger, I could have carried him up, and caught the ponies and brought him home."

"Not with a broken leg, Bob. I think you did better. You called to your King, did you not? We need never mind being weak, if we rely on the strength of the Strongest in heaven and earth. Help was brought to you, but I like to think that it was your King who sent the help, in answer to your prayer."

"Do you really think that, Mums?"

"Yes, I do."

Bob was silent for a moment, then he said emphatically:

"I'll always pray then, when I can't do things."

His mother got him to bed, and the next morning he seemed none the worse for his wetting and exposure.

Later in the day his uncle came down to the Ferry House to give a reassuring account of Harry, who was fairly well, and to see Bob.

He placed his hand on his shoulder affectionately.

"This is the second time I'm indebted to you, and this time I've really a good deal to thank you for. I think you must have saved my boy's life. He might have been drowned in that pool if you hadn't gone down and got him out. A boy was drowned there a couple of years back— lost his way as you did in a mist. It ought to be fenced in. I'll see that it is done."

"Harry would have done the same for me," said Bob a little awkwardly.

"Would he? I'm not so sure. I think he would have ridden off on his pony for help, but by the time he had got it, it would have been too late to save life. No, you've sound common sense, my boy, and thought for others before yourself. I wish Harry were more like you."

Bob looked uncomfortable, but there was a little satisfaction in his heart that he was praised and not blamed for yesterday's disaster. His sisters listened to his story breathlessly, but their pity was wholly for Harry: they did not consider that Bob had done anything out of the way.

"Poor, poor Harry!" said tender-hearted little Bee; "perhaps he'll have to lie in bed for months like Jimmy, he may never get up again."

Dew overheard this and reassured her.

"He'll soon be up and about again. Bones mend quickly when you're young!"

In a week's time Harry was able to see visitors. Bob was the first to see him, but Bee was the next, and somehow though Harry loved talking with Bob over their experiences together, he was soothed and pleased by Bee's affection and sympathy.

She patted his hand caressingly.

"You poor dear Harry! I've cried dreffully for you. When first I heard it I did, but now you're getting better, aren't you? Only it must hurt awfully. How brave you are to smile and talk with a broken leg!"

Harry made a wry face:

"I'm not brave at all. I'm an awful coward. I hate pain!"

"But it's better than being dead—at least I don't know," Bee hastily corrected herself: "Of course Jimmy was very happy when he thought he was going to die, and he told me at first he was just a little disappointed when he was told he was going to live, but now he's glad, and so am I."

"I shouldn't like to have died at all," said Harry. "It's horrible to think about."

"Oh no," said Bee with a wise shake of her head, "not if you love Jesus Christ and want to see Him."

"I don't," said Harry in a low tone.

Bee looked at him rather incredulously. Then she smiled, and patted his hand lovingly.

"You'll love Him if you think about Him," she said; "Jimmy said he thought a lot about Him, and about what He did, when He went about healing people."

"Well," said Harry slowly, "I see now that Bob is right in always helping people before you help yourself. I'm going to do like him when I get well. He's a first rate fellow, Bob is! I didn't like him much at first, and I hated him being stronger than me; but if he hadn't been, he'd never have got me out of that pool. It was awful! I couldn't get out, and I could only twist my face round, and then the water got in my mouth. I thought I was dying!"

"You poor fing!"

Bee's blue eyes were full of pity.

"And," Harry went on, being bent upon confessing his failings, "I see now that all of you are much happier than I am. And if only I get well again, I'm not going to grumble over this house being let or anything of that sort. Dad has been most awfully decent, he's talked things over with me. And I see *having* things doesn't make you great, it's *being* things, that does. I dare say I've been rather a snob. I'll try not to be."

"I do love you, Harry, now!" said Bee. "I fink you're very very brave in lying here, and talking so patient!"

Bee's praise might be a little over-done, but it was very sincere.

As Harry improved in health, he saw a great deal of his cousins, and though he was irritable and impatient, he did struggle hard to keep a brave smiling face.

Easter had come, and gone. The Hall had been let, and Harry's mother was busy in London arranging the new house. Harry's broken leg was well again, though not quite as strong as the other one. He and Bob were both being packed up for school. The little girls were rather mournful over the prospect, and the extreme cheerfulness of the boys annoyed them.

When the last day came, they were all invited to tea at the Hall. Uncle Ralph was going to take the two boys to school on the following day. When tea was over, and the children were enjoying a last ramble over the old garden, their elders sat together looking into the garden with its sweet-scented spring flowers, and wondering sadly when they would all be there again.

"But I think it will be better for Harry to be away from all this for a time," said Aunt Judy. "He was getting to consider himself a prince in possession."

"Yes," said his father; "you are right. He will find his own level at school, and learn to be content with less in life."

"Not necessarily less," said Mrs. Percival softly. "The best things in life can always be his."

Aunt Judy nodded, and her brother looked grave.

Outside, the children for the last time were sitting in Harry's wonderful nest up in the big tree at the end of the lawn.

"Fancy!" Harry was saying indignantly; "the new chap was walking round the other day, and he told Robert, the under gardener, to have all this mess cleared out of this tree as soon as we were gone!"

"He's too fat to sit in it himself," said Bob; "I saw him strutting along the other day."

"And you won't be here," said Babs; "so it won't matter. And when you come here when you're big, you'll be too big to sit in it. It's just like the birds when they get too big for the nest, they go, and the gardeners pull it down."

"Yes," said Harry gloomily; "I'm being turned out, that's right enough."

"Because you're big enough for school," said Bob cheerfully. "Mums says we shall find, as we grow up, lots of different things happen which make us happy in a different way. It sounds confusing, but I know we shall have a fine time at school. And, Harry, you can always come to the Ferry House or to Aunt Judy's in the holidays. And we'll have our ponies and picnics on the moor."

"Yes," said Harry trying to speak cheerfully, "I haven't lost my pony. Aunt Judy is going to keep him for me." Then he looked round upon his cousins.

"I'm glad to think," he said solemnly, "that you'll always be here at the Ferry House. I wanted you to come when I first heard about you, and then when I saw you I didn't care so much about you. Now it's different!"

"Yes, we love you," cried Bee in her breathless impulsive way; "we didn't like you at first, because you thought a lot of yourself. Now you don't. And Babs and me will miss you and Bob—bofe of you—dreffully! But we shall see each other in the holidays, and ride out on the moor again. And by that time Jimmy will be home, and we can all go and see him. He's really able to sit up in a chair now, and Cousin Ted has given him a chair which wheels about."

Harry was not so interested in Jimmy's recovery as Bee. He looked round the old garden from his seat in the nest, and felt rather sad, though he tried not to show it.

"There's Mother calling," he said; "we shall have to go!"

Then as they clambered out of the nest Bob waved his cap.

"Three cheers for the old nest before it goes! And for Harry too!"

The cheers were given. Harry would not be outdone.

"And three cheers for the Ferry House!" he cried, "and all who are in it."

The cheers were given, and very soon the little party broke up and separated.

Quiet dusk crept into the old gardens of the Hall. And sleep closed the eyes of the boy who had been born to so much, and to the boy and girls who had been born to so little.

But they were all learning this one lesson—that boys and girls can be truly happy without much wealth.

And that lesson of contentment can be learnt by all.